CATCHING HOPE

CATCHING HOPE

A YOUNG ADULT NOVEL

KATHY CASSEL

HPP

Haven Point Publishing, Lynn Haven, FL
Catching Hope
Copyright © 2022 by Kathy Cassel
Cover and Interior design: Diana L. Sharples

While *Catching Hope* is a work of fiction as are all the characters, many of the locations scenery, background story, and events, including natural disasters, are based on the real-life country of Haiti and its people, history, and geography."

Haven Point Publishing
Lynn Haven, FL

Paperback ISBN: 979-8-9859043-0-7
Ebook ISBN: 979-8-9859043-3-8

Summary: Four teens who are kidnapped on a trip to Haiti must work together to escape their kidnappers and journey through a country ravaged by an earthquake to be reunited with their parents/uncle and aunt.

Keywords: twins, adoptive families, teen adoption, Haiti, kidnapping, foster families, mission trips

Endorsements for Catching Hope

Catching Hope is a must-read, Christian novel for teenagers that will keep them on the edge of their seat

Kathleen Hansley
licensed independent social worker/
clinical therapist (MSW, LISW)

Kathy Cassel has written a page-turner for today's teens. Packed with adventure, suspense, drama, danger, and a surprise ending, this story will have readers on the edge of their seats. Another great book from one of my favorite authors.

Crystal Bowman
award-winning bestselling author of
more than 100 books including
I Love You to the Stars

Author Kathy Cassel has just the right amount of suspense and adventure in Catching Hope to keep you guessing to the end. I did not want to put the book down as I followed the characters through their adventures as they learned to work together while never losing hope.

Juanita Barben
elementary paraprofessional

As a professional in the social work field, I looked forward to reading Catching Hope. I was not disappointed. From page one, Kathy Cassel draws you in and takes you through a suspense filled journey of Lexi's unexpected journey on her first vacation with her forever family. The book offers hope today's teens and touches on those in foster care or adopted. A must read.

Lisa Reynolds
social worker

Unlikely heroism, surprising survival skills, and hidden compassion bubble to the surface eventually making the perfect blend of camaraderie to tackle the present and mounting adversity.

Teresa Robbins
author

Dedication:

Catching Hope is dedicated to all the Haitian children
who came home to their forever families
in the aftermath of the 2010 earthquake.

Disclaimer:

Catching Hope is a fiction story that deals with adoption from foster care. Although the main characters in this book were abused in foster care, most foster families genuinely care about the children placed with them and want the best for those children. However there are always exceptions, and abuse can take place in birth, foster, or adoptive families. If you are in a situation where you are being abused verbally or physically, speak up. You are a victim and deserve help. Talk to a trusted adult.

While Catching Hope is a work of fiction as are all the characters, many of the locations, scenery, background story, and events, including natural disasters, are based on the real-life country of Haiti and its people, history, and geography.

Acknowledgments

A special thank you to Jeanette Windle, fiction coach extraordinaire.

Thank you to Diana Sharples for an excellent cover and interior design

Thank you to Jessica Woodruff, my travel companion on many memorable trips to Haiti.

Also a special thanks to my husband, Rick, and our children who believed in this book and encouraged me in the writing of it.

Chapter One

The sound of a horn startled me awake. I struggled to a sitting position, excitement pulsing through me. I was in a large van sitting between my sixteen-year-old adoptive brother Chad and Levi, my twin, who were both still asleep. I nudged Levi until he opened his eyes and sat up. His red hair, a shade darker than mine, was tousled, and his sapphire blue eyes were sleepy. It had been a long drive from the airport to our resort on the Haitian coastline, and although I'd wanted to stay awake and take in the scenery, I drifted off.

Now we were stopped outside an ornate iron gate. Juvens, our driver, honked again, and a man in a uniform pushed a button triggering a motor to open the gate, allowing Juvens to pull through.

I turned to Levi. "Can you believe it? Us in a foreign country?"

He nodded but was silent. Handling new situations and the stress of unfamiliar places is hard for Levi. Until a year ago, my twin brother and I were bounced from foster home to foster home, never getting a forever family partly because Levi does things that make him stand out as different. The Michaels call it quirks of his autism, but other families weren't so understanding. In fact, they could be downright mean at times.

Right after our fourteenth birthday, our case manager moved Levi to a group home to help him transition into successful adult life. What really happened was he was targeted and ended up in the emergency room, where he first met Dr.

Michaels. I met Dr. Michaels during the investigation into Levi's abuse. Then the Michaels decided to add us to their family.

After many discussions, accelerated training classes, and tons of paperwork, we were adopted. Dr. and Mrs. Michaels became our parents, and in the deal, we got a brother Chad. He was adopted by the Michaels when he was six. Now he's sixteen, a year older than us. His skin is the color of caramel, and he's strong from all the sports he plays.

Our cousin Jen was in the van seat in front of me next to Mrs. M. Jen is almost seventeen. Dr. Michaels and her dad, also known as Dr. Michaels, are brothers. She isn't adopted, and she let us know the first time we met. Thankfully, she lives in Michigan, and we live in the Florida panhandle, so it's not like we hang out much.

Even after the flight from Miami and the long van ride, her blond hair was pulled up in a perfect top knot. I made a mental note to ask Mrs. M to help me do something with my wild tangle of red hair once we were settled in.

Jen scowled. "I don't know why I had to come on this trip. I would have been fine staying home alone while my parents went on their trip to Europe—their vacation which didn't include their only child."

Dr. M turned from the front passenger seat. "You'll have to take that up with your parents. They evidently wanted to spend time alone. And they thought this trip would be a good experience for you." He smiled.

Jen didn't return his smile. She stuck her earphones back into her ears, seemingly not as curious about our new accommodations as I was.

Juvens drove slowly through the resort. Small, white houses with yellow trim and blue shutters were set among palm trees. In the middle of the resort, four small swimming pools were situated around a central concrete island filled with dirt. Lush palm trees were planted in the ornamental island.

"This is where we're staying? In one of those little houses?" I could hear the wonder in my voice, and Jen didn't miss it even with earbuds in.

"Bungalows," she said. "Not little houses."

"Little houses. Bungalows. Same thing," Chad said. "Who cares anyway? Look at the sea."

I followed Chad's gaze. Waves were rolling in and crashing onto a white sand beach, stretching as far as I could see. Chad's eyes devoured the water. "I can't wait to try out those waves!"

Juvens pulled in front of a bungalow, climbed out, and walked to the back of the van. He opened the back doors where our luggage was stored. As I went to get my luggage, a movement outside the fence drew my gaze. A short, thin man with skin like dark chocolate, a white scar etched above his right eye, was watching us. He focused on Dr. M, and his eyes narrowed, a look of pure hatred filling his face. His eyes met mine, and the look of fury on his face made my heart race. I quickly turned away. Who was the man? And more importantly, why was he looking at us as though he hated us?

Chapter Two

The others were starting to unload the van, but I stood frozen. Mrs. M came to stand beside me. "Anything wrong?"

I glanced back, but the man had vanished. I hadn't imagined him, had I? Should I mention him to Mrs. M? What would I say—a guy was looking at us like he hates us? Maybe he didn't like tourists. I forced a smile. "I'm good."

Mrs. M smiled back at me. "New places can be a little overwhelming at first."

Jen rolled her eyes but didn't respond. Ignoring her, I grabbed my backpack and handed Levi his own. Still, a sense of uneasiness lingered.

Besides our own clothes and personal care items, we'd brought suitcases full of medicine and medical supplies, which were being pulled from the van.

Once the van was unloaded, Dr. M unlocked the bungalow door. I stepped in and found myself in a large, airy, yellow-and-white room with a white tile floor. Blue cushions on the wicker couch and chairs added a splash of color. The living room and kitchen were open areas, and a sliding-glass door provided a view of the water. Tranquility flooded over me.

"There are three bedrooms," Mrs. M said. She walked over to the first door and pulled it open to reveal a queen-sized bed, dresser, desk, and a full bathroom with both a tub and a shower. "This is the master bedroom. This will be Dad's and my room."

She opened the door to a pale-yellow room where twin beds sported white comforters. The curtains were open, revealing a view of the sea through the sliding-glass door.

The third room also had twin beds, but these were covered with dark-blue comforters, and the walls were white with dark-blue trim.

Mrs. M looked around the room. "Why don't Lexi and Jen take the yellow room. The boys will take this one."

Setting my suitcase on my bed, I pulled out my clothes and changed into shorts, a tank top, and flip-flops before dropping the rest into drawers. Then I walked over to the boys' room.

Chad was hurriedly placing his clothes into the dresser. He glanced up grinning as he shoved a pile of T-shirts into a drawer and pushed it closed. "I want to get in the water before lunchtime."

"Where's Levi?" I asked.

Chad looked around, then shrugged. "Dunno. He was here. He brought his suitcase in." Chad nodded at the suitcase on one of the beds.

I walked into the family room. No Levi. Had he left the bungalow? I opened the front door and looked out. Still no sign of him.

Dr. M entered the room. "Anything wrong, Lexi?"

I turned to face him. "I don't know where Levi is. He must have gone out. He probably needs to process the trip so far."

Dr. M nodded. "He'll be fine here at the resort. But go find him if you want."

I grabbed my iPad and the international phone Dr. M had given me and dropped them into my beach bag as I headed out the door. Maybe I'd have a chance to get photos once I found Levi.

I hurried down the path leading to the pool area and walked around the four joined pools, searching for any sign of a tall, skinny boy with red hair. He wasn't there, so I headed down the gravel path toward the beach. Would he go there? Chad was the one who was eager to get into the water.

Jogging down the path, I glanced toward the shoreline. In places, the water was gently lapping the shore, while in other places, waves were crashing. I spotted Levi standing at one of the calmer areas, still wearing the jeans and T-shirt he'd worn on the plane. Water was swelling around his ankles, soaking the bottoms of his pant legs, but he was unaware as he focused on the gulls overhead.

He was totally relaxed, making my heart smile. I crossed the white sand, wanting to be near Levi, but not wanting to disturb him. He'd probably already mastered the gulls' call and who knew what else. Imitating sounds was something Levi was good at—though, at times, made him stand out as different.

Pulling my iPad from my beach bag, I headed toward Levi, hoping for candid shots. I pulled off my flip-flops to walk barefoot on the warm sand before moving closer to take a picture of Levi looking out at the water. Studying the image, I couldn't help smiling. A perfect picture of a perfect day. If I'd known what was ahead, would I have felt the same?

I turned and walked the other direction down the beach, leaving Levi to his gulls. I stopped at a point where the sun shimmered across the sea in front of me. Aqua faded to turquoise to dark blue and stretched endlessly until it touched the sky. White-capped waves crashed on the shoreline, and water rushed around me. A thunderous wave broke at my feet, unexpectedly spraying me and filling my mouth with the taste of salt.

I scurried backward and hit something solid. Strong hands grasped my shoulders. I turned and looked into Dr. M's friendly eyes, which were the same color as the darker-blue water.

He pulled the red-and-white-striped towel from around his neck and handed it to me. I wiped my face and arms, then swiped at the water trickling down my legs before handing the towel back. "Thanks."

"You're welcome." He glanced down the beach to where my brother was standing. "Levi seems fine."

I nodded.

Dr. M smiled. "I'm headed to the clinic after lunch, but we have a few minutes. Do you want to stroll along the shore and see if we can find any sand dollars?"

I shrugged. "Sure."

We walked, leaving two sets of footprints side by side, his larger than mine. A rare sense of peace washed over me. I looked back to see how far I could see our footprints, but as I did, a huge wave washed ashore, erasing any sign we had walked there just moments before. I sighed.

Dr. M stopped at a cove where waves gently lapped the shoreline. He squatted and looked into the water. "Maybe we'll have better luck here where the waves are calmer."

I squatted beside him, my eyes searching.

He reached out, lifted a handful of sand, and let it shift through his fingers. A shell remained, and he handed it to me. "Not a sand dollar, but nice."

I held it on my palm and studied it. The shell was over an inch long, spiral-shaped, and had crisscrossed ridges. Dots of orange and brown made a pattern on the white shell. I ran my thumbnail along the strong ridges of the opening. "What kind is it?"

"I don't know the scientific name, but at home people call it a 'common nutmeg.'"

I closed my hand around it, savoring the rough texture.

Still squatting by the sea, Dr. M watched me, concern lining his face. "Are you okay with this? Being here in Haiti?"

I ran my thumb along the shell's ridges, up and down, up and down. "Sure."

His eyes searched my face. "It's not what I would have planned for your first vacation with us. I hadn't intended to make my annual trip to the clinic this June, but with the new outbreak of cholera, I felt compelled to come."

I shifted positions, putting one knee down on the wet sand. "I understand. In fact, I'd like to go to the clinic with you. Maybe help you with the medical care."

Dr. M didn't answer at first. He seemed to be thinking it through. "In past years, Mom and Chad have both helped at the clinic. But this year, we decided it would be better for all of you to stay at a resort. You won't be exposed to illnesses, and you will have more of a vacation. You can spend time together enjoying all the activities, and Mom will be here with you."

I bit at my bottom lip.

Dr. M searched my face. "What's bothering you?"

"I feel awkward around Jen. Chad's funny, and he likes everyone, but Jen—she doesn't understand us—what life was like for us."

He nodded. "No, she probably doesn't. I won't say I understand what you went through either, but I care."

I held up the common nutmeg, the points between my thumb and first finger. "My life has been full of bumps and ridges. But those hard times don't make a neat pattern like this."

I closed one hand around the shell, breathed in slowly through my mouth, and let the air escape the same way. "Life wasn't so bad for me. But Levi—for him it was different. Then when they separated us and put him in the group home, supposedly to help him ..."

I jumped up and brushed the sand from my legs.

Dr. M stood and opened his mouth to speak, but stopped. Instead, he pointed at the water washing ashore. "Look, there's a sand dollar. You can get it."

We squatted side by side. The sand dollar was carried out by a wave but washed ashore again a moment later. Dr. M pointed.

"Catch it."

I trickled my fingers through the water, not reaching for it, and the wave pulled it back out to sea. I glanced at Dr. M. His face was questioning.

A sigh escaped my lips. "I probably would have missed."

"It was right there in your reach."

"It's not important."

"It is if it's something you want, Lexi."

"It was probably broken anyway."

He met my gaze. "You'll never know if you don't try."

I looked down at the water lapping at my toes. "Are we still talking about sand dollars?"

He was silent. Had he heard my question? Was he merely ignoring it? Another wave washed ashore and back out before he spoke.

"I hope this trip will be more than simply a vacation for you. I hope you'll find what you're looking for."

"What I'm looking for?"

"At times, I feel like something is missing from your life."

I remained silent. What was there to say? Sure, something was missing from my life. A normal childhood, for one. I didn't know what he meant though. I couldn't get back the years I lost.

Still crouching, Dr. M took the common nutmeg from me, held it up, then handed it back. "You may not see now how the parts of your life all fit together to make a beautiful pattern. But you still have years ahead to see how God can weave the pieces of your life into something beautiful. I'm hoping you'll ask God to show you part of his plan for you on this trip."

"God will *show* me?"

"Sure. There's a verse in the Bible written to the Jews who were in exile, but I don't think God minds if we borrow the verse for ourselves. It says, 'For I know the plans I have for you,' declares the Lord, 'plans to prosper you and not to harm you, plans to give you hope and a future.' You'll find the verse in the book of Jeremiah. God knows how the pieces of our lives fit together."

"If it's true, then why does all the junk in our lives happen?"

Dr. M frowned. "I don't know. But the abuses that happened to you were because people failed you, not God."

Before I could respond, Chad ran up to us. The conversation with Dr. M was over—for now.

Chad turned to Dr. M. "When can we eat? I see people in line for the buffet."

Dr. M scrutinized Chad. "Are you monitoring your blood sugar and insulin?"

Chad nodded. "Keeping my insulin pump full, and we have plenty of extra with us."

Dr. M grinned. "Then let's find the others and join the line. I'll have to head to the clinic as soon as we finish."

"You two go on," I said. "I'll get Levi and meet you there."

"I'll go with you," Chad said.

We walked toward the shoreline to where Levi stood. "It's time for lunch," I called to my brother.

He was so caught up in listening to the gulls overhead, I couldn't tell if he'd heard me. Then a gull's cry filled the air. If I hadn't known it was Levi, I'd have thought the sound came from one of the white birds flying over the roiling waves.

Jen strolled toward us. She gawked at Levi, then turned to me. "What's he doing?"

Before I could answer, Chad laughed and said, "I think it's obvious he's making bird sounds."

Jen ignored him and focused on me. "Why is he doing that?"

I shrugged. "Just something he does."

"Really?" Her tone said more than her word.

I ignored her and approached Levi, letting him know it was time to eat. We made our way to the buffet line to join Dr. and

Mrs. M. What happened next should have been a hint of what was to come.

The buffet had a fruit table with mangoes, papayas, bananas, pineapple, strawberries, grapes, and even a watermelon, which was cut into a fancy shape. I filled a plate with fruit, then stopped at a table loaded with various meats, beans, and pasta selections before heading to our table to eat.

Rich flavors exploded in my mouth as I savored each bite. Chad caught my gaze, his mouth full of food. He swallowed and grinned. "Amazing?"

I nodded, scooped up a bite of rice smothered in a red sauce, and took a bite. Instantly, my mouth was aflame. I grabbed my water cup and gulped so fast I choked, spewing water onto the table.

Jen laughed.

I coughed, then glared at Jen. "What's so funny?"

She threw her head back and laughed more. "You are. I can tell this trip is going to be very amusing."

Heat rose in my neck. Pushing back from the table, I stood. I needed to get away from her before I reacted in an unpleasant way. I hurried across the grounds to the bungalow, putting space between us. How could I possibly share a room with her? Pulling out the key card Dr. M had given me, I slid the card in the door lock, then pushed the door open and stepped inside. That's when this trip became anything but an ordinary vacation.

My breath caught. The white wicker furniture was toppled over, and the blue cushions were on the floor. Everything was in disarray. The sliding door was open a crack. Who had done this? Had someone been here? A fist tightened in my stomach.

I glanced toward the bedrooms. The master bedroom door was ajar, and a slight sound of movement came from the room. Was the person who did this still here? Or was a breeze coming through an open window and rustling the curtain? Should I investigate or get Dr. M?

With my heart thudding in my throat, I reached into my back pocket for my phone. My pocket was empty! My phone along with my iPad was in my beach bag, which I'd left at the buffet in my hurry to get away from Jen.

I pictured the look on her face if I ran for help, and it turned out to be nothing. I didn't want to give her anything else to laugh at me for, so I swallowed my anxiety, took a breath, and slowly released it. I hoped the open sliding door meant whoever had broken in was long gone. I strode to the master bedroom and pushed the door the rest of the way open. A thin man with skin like dark chocolate, dressed in black pants and a white shirt, was bent over the bed, rifling through one of the boxes of medicine we'd brought with us.

I gasped, and he spun around to face me, his black eyes boring into my light-blue ones. There was a small, white scar above his right eye—the man I'd seen outside the gate earlier! While I stood frozen, he snatched the box from the bed and charged at the bedroom door. I screamed. What else was I, a fifteen-year-old girl, going to do face-to-face with an intruder?

Chapter Three

Instinctively, I blocked the doorway. The man wasn't much taller than my five feet, five inches, and there was no sign he had a gun. I couldn't let him take the drugs Dr. M had brought for the clinic.

The thief shoved me against the doorframe and pushed past. His strong body odor assaulted my nose, like Chad's football uniform after a game, only much worse.

"Stop! You can't have that!" I grabbed the side of the box and yanked, hoping the cardboard wouldn't tear.

The man pulled the box back to himself. He might be small, but he was strong. I tightened my grip on the box, lifted my foot, and stomped on his insole as hard as I could. My flip-flop didn't do any damage but put him off guard. I kicked off the flip-flop and smashed my heel into his knee. I had laughed when Dr. M signed me up for a four-week self-defense class for teenage girls. I wasn't laughing anymore.

"Help, thief!" I screamed.

The man faltered, and I grabbed the box, at the same time hitting him hard with my elbow in his stomach. His grasp weakened as he doubled over, and I yanked the box away.

Bottles of medicine spilled out the top, hit the floor, and rolled. The thief stood upright, nostrils flaring, his eyes narrowed and filled with hatred. As he reached for me, I jumped backward.

Voices penetrated the bungalow from the outside. I turned toward the door and yelled louder. "Help! Thief!"

The man turned, dashed toward the sliding-glass door, yanked it open, and ran out. I was still clutching the box as Dr. M and Levi, carrying my beach bag, rushed in.

Dr. M took in the scene with a sweeping glance. "Are you okay?"

I nodded, and Dr. M continued. "Levi was worried when you left so quickly without finishing lunch, so I told him we'd come check on you. Good thing too. What happened?"

Levi mutely handed me my beach bag as I told them about finding the family room torn apart and seeing the bedroom door ajar. Levi was biting at his bottom lip by the time I finished. "You okay?"

Making my smile as assuring as possible, I answered, "I hurt him more than he hurt me!"

Levi grinned, but Dr. M was less than happy with my explanation. He said sternly, "You should have left as soon as you saw this room. You could have been hurt."

"I didn't know someone was still here stealing your stuff." I didn't add the part about not wanting to make a mistake in front of Jen.

"If he works here, he may know I'm a doctor. He might have been looking for medicine he could sell on the black market. Or he might only have been a common thief looking for anything small enough to steal and hit the jackpot with the medications."

I told Dr. M about seeing the man outside the gate while we were unloading, bringing even more concern to his face.

Dr. M pulled out his cell phone. "I'm going to call security, and they can call the police. Lexi, you'll need to give a report and a description of the man."

Chad burst into the room, followed by Mrs. M and Jen. He looked around. "Whoa. Lexi, you do this?"

"No! Why would I do this?"

"You looked pretty angry when you left the table."

My mouth dropped open. "You think I would do this?"

Chad looked around, then grinned. "Nah, guess not. It would be a little overkill when you could simply dump Jen's clothes in the swimming pool or something."

"Grow up!" Jen said. "Uncle David, what happened here?"

Dr. M quickly explained. He'd no sooner finished than a security guard arrived. After asking a few brief questions, he phoned the police.

Once the police arrived, I recounted the whole story again and described the man in detail. The police wrote down what I said. Both the police and hotel security guard promised to keep an eye out for anyone suspicious.

Once they'd gone, Dr. M grew serious. "Chad, Jen, Lexi, Levi, it's important you be alert even while here at the resort. What happened earlier shouldn't happen again, but the man entered the resort once, so he's either someone they know or someone who knows how to get in."

Jen sighed loudly. "We get it! We'll be careful! Now if we're done with all this drama, can we go shopping or something? I don't want to hang around here. Or if no one else wants to go out, I could grab a cab."

"You won't find the kind of stores you're used to near here," Mrs. M said.

Dr. M faced Jen. "And you can't go out shopping alone anyway. You need to have one of us with you unless you are on one of the planned excursions or with a resort driver like Juvens, who drove us from the airport."

"So why did we come if we're going to be stuck here?" Jen pouted. "What are we supposed to do all day?"

Mrs. M smiled. "They have beach volleyball, beach soccer, basketball, snorkeling, swimming, kayaking, tennis, and I've heard they are even setting up a huge water trampoline tomorrow. I'm sure, with all those choices, we can find something fun to do together."

Jen rolled her eyes. "I don't plan to get all sweaty or play on a beach trampoline with the little kids. There's nothing for me to do but tan by the pool, and I'm not staying there all day. It's too hot. Can't I get one of the hotel drivers to take me to the mall? It's not the first time I've been in a foreign country."

Dr. M faced her. "Haiti is different. We've come to expect the unexpected here—kidnappings, hurricanes, even a serious earthquake several years back. You saw the damage on the way here from the airport."

Jen's mouth dropped open. "If we could get kidnapped or be in a hurricane, why are we here?"

"The country of Haiti is always struggling. They need help, and we can do our part of helping. I'll be at the clinic a lot of the time, but Aunt Maggie will be here with you. If she has to come to the clinic with me, you can join in any of the activities the resort has planned."

"Sure. Activities like beach volleyball or bouncing on a water trampoline. No thanks! At least I have my iPad and MP3 player."

Dr. M began packing up the boxes of medicine for the cholera patients. Soon the resort van pulled up with Juvens at the wheel. Dr. M climbed in beside him, waving goodbye through a rolled-down window. "Enjoy yourselves, kids. I should be back by dinner."

As the van headed toward the resort exit, I wandered outside. Walking slowly along the shore where I'd looked for shells earlier with Dr. M, I found a dry place on the sand. Spreading my towel, I lowered myself onto it.

Typing my pass code into my iPad, I opened my journal. I wanted to attempt my own creativity. On the internet, I'd found out how to take a photo, save it, then outline the image by writing words. I'd been experimenting with different colors and fonts.

I considered writing about the thief but didn't want to think about him. I hoped his face wouldn't haunt my dreams. Pulling the common nutmeg from my pocket, I rolled it between my thumb and finger, then sat it on the sand in front of me. I took a close-up photo of the shell and saved it to my journal before studying the sea where the shell had originated.

June 4
Turquoise water reaches toward the sky.
Sun glints off white sand as waves lap at my feet.
A sand dollar swirls in and swirls out.
A shell washes ashore.
Where have they been?
The aqua depth teams with life far below the surface.
A hidden world.
Freedom.

"Are you okay?" Mrs. M's voice interrupted my thoughts. I looked up at her. She was wearing navy-blue walking shorts, a white scoop-neck T-shirt, and navy sandals. Her thick, dark hair was pulled back into a ponytail. Blue eyes gazed at me from a suntanned face. She was beautiful without even trying.

"Sure, I'm fine."

She lowered herself to the sand next to me with a laugh. "Of course. Merely another ordinary day. Flying to a new country. Being exposed to new foods and a new language. Oh, and then there's the matter of tackling a thief and keeping him from taking the life-saving medication for the clinic."

I grinned, even though I tried not to. "Okay. This first day in Haiti has been a little out of the ordinary, but I wouldn't change anything. I've never done anything like this before."

"I should hope not."

"I meant going on vacation, not discovering a thief. That was like out of a movie or something."

Mrs. M nodded toward my iPad. "What are you doing? Taking pictures?"

I shrugged. "It's nothing. Just something I'm trying to do. Writing words around the shape of the picture."

"May I see?"

My face flushed. "I'm not good at it. I'm trying to ..."

To what? Record my thoughts? Be creative?

Mrs. M smiled ruefully. "It's okay. I can be too nosy. You can tell me to back off."

"No. It's not you. I'm just messing around." I showed her my journal. "See, I'm taking photos of cool stuff I see—scenery, close ups, and then I try to fit the words around the photos. Not poetry because it doesn't have any real pattern, only my observations."

I showed her the one of the shell. She turned it, reading slowly. I studied her expression, trying to figure out what she thought, but I couldn't tell. Even though I was only keeping the journal for myself, I wanted her to like it.

Mrs. M looked up at me and smiled. "This is good, Lexi. You have a way with words. You not only describe what you see, but you convey feelings too."

Warmth crept up my neck at the unexpected praise. "Thank you. It's ... just something I'm trying. I think it might be fun to be a photographer or a writer."

"Then you should go for it. You have three more years of high school. You can take photos for the yearbook or write for the paper."

"You think so?"

"Sure, and I'll help you any way I can." She stood and put out a hand to pull me up. "But for now, let's see what the others are doing."

We headed back to the bungalow. No sooner than we entered, Chad bounded through the door. "They're going to play volleyball on the beach. Anyone want to play?"

After volleyball, we all swam in the pool until late afternoon when Dr. M returned from the clinic.

Chapter Four

As we approached the dining area, the music grew louder—lively tunes making my heart dance. I caught a glimpse of the musicians. Five men were playing what looked like homemade instruments—two guitars, one banjo, a wooden drum, and brightly painted maracas.

I didn't know what the style of music was called, but it was upbeat and lively and cast a festive spell on me. The others' smiles told me they felt the same.

I turned on my iPad and snapped a picture. The photo didn't catch the mood, so I switched to video and began recording the band and even some of the spectators. I zoomed in on the maraca player to capture his energy and smile.

Chad, moving nearer to the musicians, began an impromptu dance beside them. He saw me and grinned, motioning for me to take a video of him. How could he be so carefree? I was both curious and jealous. I wanted the freedom to join in and not worry about what anyone thought. I took several short videos he could post to his social media accounts or send to friends.

A movement at the edge of the crowd caught my eye. The skin on the back of my neck prickled. I turned and peered into the shadows. No one was there. I was being ridiculous. With all the people milling around, of course I'd seen movement. The encounter with the thief earlier had spooked me!

I didn't realize how soon I'd see him again, or what a major part he'd play in everything that happened during this trip.

"Lexi." Dr. M broke into my thoughts. He took my iPad. "Your turn. I'll take the pictures."

I hesitated. I wanted to join Chad, but my feet wouldn't move. Chad reached out and pulled me into the circle of musicians. I wasn't sure what to do, but the maraca player handed me his maracas, and after a few seconds of hesitation, I shook them to the beat of the music. Soon I forgot about Dr. M videoing and the others watching, and I let myself flow with the music until the song ended.

I started to hand the maracas back, but Dr. M slipped the man a few bills folded together and pushed the maracas into my hands.

I gave him questioning look. "If I keep these, what will he play?"

Dr. M nodded at a pile of maracas mostly out of sight near the man's feet. "He has extra to sell tourists. It's part of his income."

"I—thank you," I stammered. I studied the maracas. They were bright yellow with red flowers and green leaves weaving around in a circle.

Dr. M looked at the others. "Does anyone else want a pair?"

Levi shook his head as Chad said, "I have a pair from the Haitian mission already."

Dr. M turned to Jen. "Jen?"

"Maracas? Really?" Jen said. "When I go on vacation with my parents we buy ..."

"A bunch of expensive stuff. We know, Jen!" Chad said. "But the maracas are cool. Let Lexi enjoy them."

I was starting to feel awkward, but just then Mrs. M joined us, and we went to get into the line for the buffet.

By the time we finished eating, threads of red and orange were beginning to streak the sky. I headed to the beach and set my maracas on the sand. I took a photo for my journal and tapped the screen to add descriptive words.

June 4
Harmony and melody dance
under the skillful hands of Haitian musicians.
There's a song in my feet,
and they want to dance along.
Singing, laughing,
White skin and caramel among dark chocolate.
Beauty for the heart. Music for the soul.
A cacophony of culture and heritage.

Two hours later, I dropped into bed exhausted, sure I'd go right to sleep, but my mind kept going over the day's events. I finally fell asleep after midnight. When I woke up the next day, Dr. M had already left for the clinic. I spent most of the day walking on the beach, taking photos, and swimming.

The following days were the same—walking, swimming, reading books I'd downloaded to my iPad. In only three days, we'd fallen into a routine. Jen would claim a lounge chair by one of the pools and spend the day there. The rest of us would take part in the sports, or Levi would go off by himself to explore something that had caught his attention. He'd research it on his iPad until he knew every little detail, whether a bird, a shell, or the history of something in Haiti. And every night Mrs. M would unload the pocketful of stuff he'd acquired during the day. Most people would have discarded his collection as trash, but Mrs. M put everything in a small box for the trip home.

On my fourth morning at the resort, I walked along the beach, letting the steady cadence of the waves lull my spirits. If only life could always be this carefree and peaceful. I dropped to the sand, sitting so my toes were lapped at by the waves. Levi came and sat beside me, holding out his iPad.

"There's a mission near La Visite National Park—and a fort."
The tone in his voice alerted me I would soon know more

about the mission than I wanted to know. I glanced at the web page as he continued, "It was founded as a Christian mission, but it also has a trade school so the poor can learn to sew, bake, cook, make items from wood, or create jewelry to support themselves. They sell the stuff in a shop there."

"Like a gift shop?"

"And a bakery and restaurant. Do you think we can go if one of the drivers can take us?"

"Sounds interesting. We can ask."

A shadow fell across us, and I looked up. It was Mrs. M. Perfect timing.

"We were hoping to find you," I said. "Levi has been reading about a mission here. Would we be able to visit it?"

"The mission? Oh, sure. We try to go there at least once each time we visit Haiti. We often go to Fort Jacques on the same trip. In fact, the mission might be a solution to a situation that came up."

"What situation?"

"Dad needs me at the clinic. The cholera epidemic is affecting many more people now, and they are walking or coming by tap-tap, those brightly colored trucks you saw on the way from the airport to the clinic for medical care. He's trying to start the most critical patients on IVs for hydration and on antibiotics, but he needs more help. I was going to go see what I could do."

"Can we help?" I asked.

"No, that's not necessary. The resort offers an excursion to the mission, so maybe we can arrange for you to go. Why don't we find the others and make a plan?"

A few minutes later, we were sitting around a table by the pool while Mrs. M explained the plan.

Chad's face lit up. "Awesome!" He turned to us. "You start smelling cinnamon rolls before you even get inside."

I grinned, ready to respond, but Jen broke in. "Are you even allowed to have them with your diabetes?"

Chad's smile faltered for a second, but Mrs. M answered. "Yes, if he's careful about his insulin." She turned to him. "Make sure to take bottled water and extra insulin with you."

Then Mrs. M turned to Jen. "You wanted to shop. You can buy souvenirs like jewelry or handmade shirts or carvings for your parents and help support the men and women who are in training there."

Jen rolled her eyes. "Just what I wanted to do."

Chad turned to her. "Don't be ugly, Jen. It's a good idea."

She shrugged.

Chad grinned. "Good. Then we're going. Get us a driver."

Mrs. M raised her eyebrows.

"Please. There was an unspoken please on that sentence," Chad added hurriedly.

Mrs. M smiled at him and looked at each of us. "You'll stay together and follow the driver's instructions, right?"

Chad's brows furrowed. "Of course. Safety first, but the fort does have a dungeon ..."

Mrs. M tried to look stern but ended up grinning. "No locking anyone in the dungeon. I'll go talk to the activities director and see if we can arrange this. Gather what you need—snacks, water bottles."

I nodded and left to pack my backpack. I traded my flip-flops for my sneakers in case we had to do a lot of walking. This would be the best day ever.

I couldn't stop smiling.

I took a picture of my backpack.

June 7
Excited, ready to go.
On our way to the mission.

Chad wants cinnamon rolls.
I want a new experience.
Will I find what Dr. M says is missing?
I hope so!

Chapter Five

An hour later, we were climbing into the same van in which we'd traveled from the airport, Juvens again at the wheel. Mrs. M had insisted we each pack two bottles of water, protein bars, spending money, and money enough to get home in case we had to find alternative transportation. My backpack also contained my iPad and phone, secured in a built-in, padded waterproof pouch. Chad and Levi also had backpacks while Jen carried a name-brand bag covered with bright flowers.

Before we left, Mrs. M did a whole safety briefing with us, talking about situations I'd never thought about. Jen made a big show of indignation because Mrs. M didn't think her trips to fancy places gave her the knowledge to travel safely in Haiti. She showed impatience at such information as "sit behind the driver because he can't pull a gun on you if you're sitting behind him" and "have a designated meeting place in case you get separated."

While I didn't share Jen's feelings, I found myself wondering why such protocols would even matter when the resort driver was taking us to the mission.

When Juvens pulled up in the van, Jen pushed ahead to grab the front passenger seat, announcing, "I want more leg room."

That her decision left Chad, who really could use more leg room, cramped against the far window behind Juvens clearly never crossed Jen's self-centered mind. I followed Chad into the second row, while Levi climbed into the back row. Chad talked animatedly as we pulled out of the gate and away from the resort. "I can't wait for you guys to see this place. It's got everything. Ice cream, fries, donuts, rolls."

Jen gave an exaggerated sigh. "Don't you think about anything but food? Are you sure you can have all that food at once?"

"Yes. With my insulin pump if I'm careful not to overdo. I brought extra insulin like Mom said. Changed batteries too. But there are products besides food. The items the people make in classes like jewelry or wood carvings or ..."

"Like I care," Jen interrupted.

Chad's eyes narrowed.

I interrupted before he could say anything to Jen. "Tell me about the area. Where are we exactly?"

The smile returned to Chad's face. "The mission isn't far from us, but there aren't any direct roads, so we'll be winding through the mountains. The mission is southeast of the resort, but the clinic where Mom and Dad are is almost straight south of us."

"Maybe I can get good scenery photos," I said. "Photos at the mission too."

"Definitely," Chad said. "You'll see the Haitians at work making the products to sell. If you want real life pictures, ask to watch the men cooking or baking."

"We can do that?"

"Sure. They encourage visitors to look around and see what goes on there. You might take some interesting photos."

It was growing hot in the van, and Juvens turned on the air conditioning. We were now on a small, seemingly nameless road in the mountains. I tried to open the maps program on my iPad, but there was no internet service. I sighed.

"What?" Chad asked.

"I wanted to follow our route on my iPad to know where we

are."

"We are following a road north of the Rivie're Frorse," Juvens said from the front. "It may not appear on a map."

"Probably be faster to take a boat," Jen muttered. "We'll never get there at this speed."

"It's worth the trip. Look at these mountains," Chad said.

Jen opened her mouth to say something, but I cut in. "Let me guess. You've seen loftier mountains in some grand place you've been with your parents."

"Well, yes, I have seen a few of the most famous mountain ranges like the Veysonnaz where we ski in Valais, Switzerland and ..."

Shaking my head, I interrupted again before we had to listen to an entire list. "Yeah, I figured!"

"Look at all the different kinds of trees," Chad put in, heading off a full-blown squabble. "Bet you don't see foliage and trees like this in Michigan."

Jen shifted her scornful frown to her cousin. "We have lots of forests in Michigan, but it's not like I go camping or anything."

I pulled out my iPad and set it for camera. The mountains and various plants were interesting. I zoomed in on a bird flying over the tall trees.

Chad watched me. "How did the videos of me with the musicians turn out?"

"Oh! I forgot all about them." I clicked on my video files and found the ones of Chad. "Let's watch them."

I clicked play, and the festive music filled the van. Chad leaned in from one side, and Levi from over the seat to watch the video. I grinned as I relived Chad dancing side by side with the Haitians. Then a movement at the far left of the video clip caught my eye. When the video ended, I skipped back to the point where I'd seen it.

"What are you looking for?" Chad asked.

"Probably nothing." Pausing the video, I used my thumb and forefinger to enlarge the shot where I spotted movement. My breath caught as a man's face emerged from the shadows at the very edge of the iPad screen. He was staring straight at the camera, hatred in his glare, his mouth twisted into a snarl. I let out a small gasp as I zoomed in closer on a small, white scar. I hadn't been imagining it. The thief really had been watching me!

Chapter Six

"What is it, Lexi?" Chad's words broke into my thoughts. "Who's that?"

"The man there in the shadows. He's the one who broke into the bungalow and tried to steal the medicine. See the scar? But why would he be back on the resort property? And why is he staring at me like that?"

I forced myself to take a deep breath and release it slowly. The man was only a video. He wasn't watching me now.

"Maybe he isn't staring at you. You merely happened to catch him on camera." Concern lined Chad's face. "Still, if he really is the thief, we definitely need to let Dad and Mom know he's still around. This isn't a coincidence. You need to show them the video as soon as we get back to the resort."

I nodded. "I will, but it's kind of creepy. Why does he keep showing up?"

Chad shrugged. "Maybe he doesn't realize the drugs aren't at the resort anymore, and he still thinks he has a chance at stealing them."

The van suddenly braked, causing me to glance up. Ahead, a truck was stopped in the road. A slightly built Haitian man was wrestling a rear tire loose. Shifting gears to idle, Juvens turned around to look back at me.

"You mentioned the man who broke into your bungalow. I was told of the incident. Since we will be waiting some time before the truck moves, may I see the picture? It would be useful to know what the thief looks like."

I passed my iPad to Juvens. He studied the image. "I don't recognize him. Certainly he is not an employee at the resort nor any guest I have seen. If this is indeed the thief, you must show this picture to police."

Juvens handed me back the iPad, then opened the driver's door. "I will help the truck driver with his tire so we can get going."

"I'll help too," Chad said.

"Me too," Levi chimed in.

While the guys followed Juvens over to where the truck driver was changing his tire, I climbed out to take a few pictures of the mountainous area. We were soon on our way again. As we drove through a town with rows of small houses, several small stores, and even a church, Chad announced, "We'll be there soon."

Sure enough, a few minutes later, Juvens pulled into the gravel parking lot in the front of a gift shop. I could see shelves with merchandise on them. I climbed out of the van, thankful the ride was over.

But if I'd known what was ahead, what would I have done differently? Was there anything else I could have done?

"Please meet back here at the van in two hours," Juvens said. "I will be around back with the other drivers. If you need anything, you find me."

I followed Chad across the stone patio to a brick building. Large glass windows and doors allowed us to see rows of carved items even before we went in. As Juvens strode around the side of the building, Chad opened the door and gestured for us to enter.

Stepping inside, I glanced around the gift shop. A hint of disappointment edged in. The store was more modern than I'd expected. I had pictured a cinderblock and tin-roofed shop like many shops we'd passed on the way here, and I was looking forward to seeing something more native and less tourist-oriented than this.

I shrugged, focusing on the store. It was small with a tiled floor and white walls. Merchandise was carefully displayed on shelves. On the top shelves, little carved wooden boxes shaped like turtles were stacked alongside ships, animals, bowls, and globes. Below them were larger boxes and bowls and even trunks with intricate designs carved on them.

I turned from the carved items to the painted metal geckos and flowers hanging on the wall, realizing the $20 Mrs. M had given me wasn't going to go as far as I hoped. I'd have to shop carefully. Jen, of course, had her own money and lots of it, as she let us know.

I glanced over to see her fingering handmade necklaces. She turned and saw me looking at her, then hung the necklaces back on the rack and walked away.

I glanced around to see where Levi was. He and Chad were both studying knives. I ambled over. Chad held up a folding knife. "I like this one—with a knife, screwdriver, pliers, and bottle opener. I think I'm going to get it. I'll have to pack it in my checked luggage on the trip home, so it won't get confiscated as a weapon."

"That's not handmade," I pointed out.

"No, but this leather case is." Chad held up a sheath decorated with detailed designs.

We spent a while longer looking around before we all finalized our choices. Levi chose a knife similar to Chad's. I finally decided on a small carved box, and Jen selected a similar box for her mom and a knife for her dad. She dropped them into the flowered bag she'd brought along.

As we walked to the cash register to pay for our stuff, Levi picked up a small plastic case with a carabineer and cord. He opened the case and poured several small items into his hand.

"What's that?" I asked.

"Fire starter kit."

"Cool," Chad said, taking the contents from Levi. He held up several small cellophane packs. "Sealed wetfire tinder pieces."

"What's a wetfire tinder?" I asked.

Chad shrugged. "Don't know, but Dad has used them before on our trips. They're white squares, and you shave a bit off."

He held up two small, plastic, orange pieces that resembled thumb drives. One had a piece of metal attached, and the other had a piece of flint fastened to it. "Then you strike the metal piece and the flint piece together to make a spark which ignites the shavings. You can plug the halves together for storage."

He handed the items back to Levi. "Are you going to buy it?"

Levi nodded as he put everything back in the waterproof case and held it by the carabineer.

Jen rolled her eyes. "Oh great. Something else for him to fasten to his belt loops."

"It's awesome. I'm getting one too," Chad said, taking a waterproof fire starter case from the rack.

Levi dropped his knife and fire starter kit on the counter along with a box of tea. I looked at him. "Tea? You don't drink tea."

"It's for Mom and Dad," he said.

Mom and Dad? When had he started calling them Mom and Dad? We'd always called them Dr. M and Mrs. M.

We each paid for our selections and headed out the door.

Chad turned to me. "Let's walk down to the work area. You can get photos of the Haitian people carving, sewing, and doing other activities. Then we'll go to the restaurant. Afterward, maybe we can get Juvens to stop at the fort on the way home."

"Why would we want to see a fort?" Jen asked, her tone condescending.

Chad frowned. "It's an important place. The Haitians built

the fort after they got their freedom from France. Every year they have a celebration there on Haitian Flag Day, May 18, three days after my birthday. Besides, you get a good view of the Bay of Port au Prince."

He turned to me. "It would give you a chance to get good photos."

"I'd like to see it," I said as we followed Chad down a stone staircase leading to a courtyard with flowers and vegetables growing all around. In the distance, covered greenhouses filled several acres of land. The courtyard was cooler here than the upstairs level. Sweet fragrances mingled with more earthy smells as we made our way into a smaller courtyard filled with bright flowering marigolds and several varieties of flowers I didn't recognize.

After watching Haitians working in the gardens, making jewelry from cereal boxes, and carving sturdy boxes and bowls from wood, we climbed the stairs to the back of the gift shop and restaurant. I glanced around. "Where's Juvens? Aren't our two hours up yet?"

Chad glanced at his watch. "We have time left. He's probably still with his friends. Let's go into the restaurant and keep an eye out for Juvens from there."

We went into a large, airy room with a white tile floor and small booths. A chalkboard listed the food choices—burgers, pizza, and soft-serve ice cream. I frowned. "I wanted Haitian food. We can get this at home."

"We'll have Haitian cuisine tonight," Chad said. "Let's get burgers for now."

My disappointment was forgotten as a large, juicy burger was placed in front of me. I was hungrier than I realized, and the meat was perfect. Only Jen opted for a salad over a hamburger.

Chad wolfed his food down, then purchased a dozen frosted

cinnamon rolls from the bakery. Dropping the box on our table, he took one out and gave an exaggerated sniff, then took a big bite and chewed with deliberate slowness.

Jen wrinkled her nose. "You're going to eat one of those after eating a whole burger?"

Chad ignored her. He was obviously enjoying the roll, so I reached across the table, pulled off a piece, and popped it into my mouth. The sweetness filled all my senses with goodness.

Chad grinned, frosting dripping down his chin. "Amazing, isn't it?"

Pulling out my iPad, I took a picture of Chad, messy face and all, then took a photo of each of us. There was no time to add text to the photos, but I jotted down a few random lines to add later.

June 7
Haitian Mission
Full of life.
Vibrant colors.
Cacophony of sounds.
Explosions of taste.
Plants growing.
Rolls baking.
People singing, talking, laughing.
Purpose fulfilled.
Lives changed.

By the time I finished, Chad was swallowing the last bite of his cinnamon roll. "Anyone else for one of these?"

When we all shook our heads, he stuffed the box with the remaining cinnamon rolls into his backpack and stood up. "Then we'd better find Juvens and head back, especially if we're going to stop at the fort before dark."

Tucking my iPad deep into my backpack, I stood up and took one more look around. "I wish Mrs. M could have come with us. I know she's seen everything before, but this is amazing. If we come back next year, I want to get one of those trunks."

"Let Mom know, and she'll make it happen," Chad grinned. "When I want something, I start talking about how the mission helps the Haitians learn a trade and support their families. She ends up buying more than she planned every time."

Gathering up our packages, we made our way outside. There was still no sign of Juvens. "Let's go to the van," Chad said. "He must be waiting there."

We walked to the van, and as Chad predicted, we found Juvens sitting in the driver's seat. Tension lined the resort employee's face as he glanced at his watch. "You are late. It is past two hours."

"We looked for you before we went inside to eat, but didn't see you," Chad said.

"I was where I said to meet."

"We looked, honest," I said.

"We will not worry anymore. Get in. We must get going."

Why was he so upset? Was he supposed to have already returned to the resort to drive someone else on an excursion? Chad once again scooted all the way across the second row, directly behind Juvens. I climbed in next. This time Levi squeezed in beside me instead of climbing into the back. Jen took her place in front again, although more hesitantly. I wasn't the only one who'd picked up on Juvens's displeasure.

Once we were in and the door shut, Juvens turned the key, quickly put the van in gear, and pulled out of the parking lot.

"Juvens, do you think we could make a quick stop at Fort Jacques?" Chad said. "I don't want the others to leave Haiti without at least getting a look."

Juvens shook his head. "The fort is closed to visitors. There was much damage over the years since the 2010 earthquake."

"I know," Chad said. "But I checked online. The park website says the interior fort is closed off, but we can still go up and at least walk around the fort, catch the view of the city."

Juvens seemed to be thinking, then shrugged. "So long as we do not stay long. No one is allowed up there after dark."

The driver maneuvered the van onto the dirt lane. The road swung around one tight curve, then another. Where the road straightened out, a man was standing beside the road. His wide-brimmed hat was tilted forward, obscuring his face. Juvens braked as the man stepped suddenly forward into the road, waving his arms.

"What is it?" Jen called out anxiously from the front seat. "You're not going to stop, are you? I don't think Uncle David would be pleased if you picked up a stranger while you are driving us."

"No worries. Of course, I am not stopping," Juvens said, swerving at a slow crawl to miss the waving man.

Suddenly, I heard a click behind me. Nothing in the van I could think of would make that kind of noise, so I instinctively turned around to identify the sound. I sucked in my breath as I caught sight of a young Haitian man, probably not much older than me, climbing over the third-row seat from the baggage compartment where he must have been hiding. He was wearing a black T-shirt and baseball cap, and in his right hand was a gun—pointed right at me!

Chapter Seven

I shrieked. By now both Levi and Chad had reacted to the sound as well, turning in their seats. Levi shrank back, but Chad surged up from his seat, grabbing at the gun.

"What are you doing? Are you crazy? He'll shoot you!" I cried out.

Thankfully, the young man had already retreated out of Chad's reach, right behind Levi, The gun was now aimed at Chad. Clearly realizing how reckless he'd been, Chad subsided into his seat, but his glare didn't leave the intruder. By now Juvens had brought the van to a complete halt. Looking his direction, the young man said something in Creole.

I looked over at Chad. "What did he say?"

It was Juvens who responded. "He said to go back and pick up the man by the road."

"No!" Jen cried out frantically. "You can't do that! Can't you see the man must be working with this guy?"

"The man behind you has a gun. He says 'go back,' I go back." Already, Juvens was reversing until the front passenger side of the van was parallel to the man standing in the road. His wide-brimmed hat still tilted to shade his face, the man yanked open the passenger door and spoke to Juvens in Creole.

Juvens turned to Jen. "You get in back with the others. He is going to sit here."

Jen climbed out of the front seat, pulled open the side door, and climbed in, but she continued to talk, addressing her angry remarks at Juvens. "Some driver you are! The resort said you were trained to protect their guests on excursions. You didn't even think to keep an eye out for someone sneaking into your van?"

"That was indeed careless, for which I am most deeply sorry. Perhaps I dozed off when you were so late." Juvens attempted to look contrite, but I caught an angry flash in the glance he gave Jen before he shrugged and said, "What is done is done. What matters now is these men have guns, so they make the rules. If they say 'drive,' I drive to keep us all from getting shot."

The man from beside the road was now climbing into the front seat, and I could see he too had a gun in his hand, which he pointed at Juvens. Only after he had pulled his door shut did he turn toward us and push his hat back. I gasped again as I found myself staring at the same white scar and hate-filled glare I'd seen in my parents' room and on my iPad screen.

From the satisfied sneer that twisted the man's lips, he knew I'd recognized him. "So we meet again," he said in accented but fluent English. "And this time things will not go so well for you. Now before we begin, you will please hand all your backpacks and bags to my nephew behind you. Stevens, you will remove any wallets and phones as well.

I felt lightheaded, my heart racing as I obeyed. Chad's jaw was tight with frustration as he passed his wallet, phone, and backpack over the back of the seat. Levi looked ready to cry as he followed suit. His belongings were important to him, just as each thing in his pockets was. I hoped they didn't make us empty our pockets.

The young man named Stevens already had Chad's backpack open and was rummaging through the contents. He pulled out Chad's wallet and rifled through the remaining money. Dropping the wallet, he pulled out the box of cinnamon rolls. Taking a sniff, he grinned and said something in Creole.

His uncle scowled and answered harshly. Stevens quickly

dropped the box onto the seat, zipped up Chad's backpack, then tossed it and the others into the luggage compartment. With the gun still leveled at us above the seat back, he opened the box of cinnamon rolls. Pulling one out, he took a huge bite, smearing his hands and face with frosting.

I swallowed back disgust. When Chad had been covered in icing, it was funny. But a practically grown young man waving a gun at us while covered in frosting like a toddler—nothing humorous about it.

The thief's nephew must have sensed my feelings—or maybe they showed on my face—because he looked right at me, took another bite, and smirked. He lost the smirk as his uncle barked out a few phrases in Creole. Dropping the roll, Stevens set down his gun, used his T-shirt to wipe his mouth and hands, then reached over the back of the seat into the luggage compartment. He pulled out a roll of silver duct tape.

"Clasp your hands in front of you," the scarred man ordered.

Stevens bound our hands with the duct tape, starting with Jen, who had to crouch down by the side door as there was no room to squeeze into the second row with the rest of us. Levi, Chad, and I had to turn around and hold our clasped hands up for Stevens to wrap our wrists with the duct tape, using a knife to cut the remaining tape.

I cringed as his sticky hands touched mine, a memory from foster care invading my memories of boys grabbing me, poking at me, and Levi charging at them to get them to stop. The largest boy held Levi while the other punched him in the stomach until he threw up.

My emotions spiraled downward as Stevens finished his task, picked up his gun again, and Juvens began to drive. Anyone we passed would see us sitting in a resort van and assume we were rich foreigners on vacation. Even if we could somehow get their attention, no one would realize our hands were bound and guns were pointed at us.

Jen was still muttering angrily, as though she still believed our captors didn't understand English. "You can't do this to us! We are American citizens! Wait until our embassy hears about this! Do you know what they do to people who kidnap Americans? You are going to end up in jail for the rest of your lives!"

Still pointing his gun at Juvens, the scarred man swiveled to grin nastily at Jen. "You Americans always think you are so powerful! You know nothing! And if you keep talking, I will tape your mouth too."

He turned his attention to me, still grinning nastily. "As for you, you have cost me much money—not to mention my foot still hurts. But I do not care because now, instead of money for drugs, I will get a big ransom."

At his continued smirk, my anger simmered, giving me courage. "Those drugs are for the clinic, for people who need them, not a thief!"

His grin faded into a furious glare as he hissed, "Don't speak of the clinic to me! Those people owe me. They have stolen ten years of my life, and now they will pay, or the American doctor and his wife will not see their children again. Four children are worth much money, yes?"

I drew in my breath for an angry response, then broke off as Chad nudged me with his foot. "Be quiet. Don't make this any worse," he whispered.

I suddenly realized I'd acted as stupidly as Jen, mouthing off at a kidnapper, or like Chad, going for his gun earlier. Levi seemed to be the only one of us who was acting sensibly.

I forced myself to take a deep breath and slowly released it. My momentary anger started to fade, fear taking its place. This man and his nephew were thieves, kidnappers, and who knew what else. Dr. and Mrs. M wouldn't even know anything was wrong until they got home from the clinic this evening and discovered we weren't there. Who knew where we'd be by then? I'd been so excited to travel somewhere new, but now I'd give anything to be back home.

Still, I couldn't help but wonder what he meant by, "They have stolen ten years of my life, and now they will pay?" Whatever he meant, it wasn't good.

Levi's eyes were now shut, his freckles standing out on his pale face. He was muttering, "Ne Neon, Na Sodium, Mg magnesium ..." Quoting random stuff when feeling stressed was another quirk of his autism.

Jen glared at him and sighed dramatically. Ignoring her, Levi started reciting louder. "Cl chlorine, Ar argon, K potassium ..."

The van jolted sharply side to side. Looking out the window, I saw we were fording a river crossing. Once across, the van began a bumpy ascent, and we had a hard time keeping our balance with our hands taped together. We drove through the mountains for what seemed hours on narrow, winding dirt roads. In reality, the drive was probably no more than thirty minutes and not many kilometers.

The van finally slowed, then braked to a stop outside a wrought-iron gate. The nephew jumped out, tugging the gate open. Juvens drove through the gate, pulling up next to a small black car with a dented front fender. Climbing out, the scarred man opened the side door of the van. "Get out!" he ordered.

Getting out was easier said than done. We were crammed together, and with our hands bound, exiting was hard to maneuver. Jen climbed out first, wobbling frantically to keep her balance. Levi followed more gracefully. As I stepped down after him, I stumbled. Tumbling from the van, I landed hard on the ground. The scarred man grabbed my arm and yanked me up. Pain shot through my shoulder, and I bit my bottom lip to keep from crying out.

Now out of the van, I looked around. The property was enclosed by a tall, black metal fence. A brick path, overgrown with thick grass, led toward a large, three-story house. Once grand, it now showed signs of neglect. Bricks were crumbling, and numerous barred windows were broken. A garden, formerly elegant, now held only a few rose bushes choked by weeds. The old mansion certainly didn't look as though anyone still lived here.

Looking around curiously, Chad asked the question on my own mind. "Whose house is this?"

"Not your concern. They left long ago when the earthquake hit, choosing not to fix the damage." Gun still raised, the kidnapper motioned for us to go ahead of him up the path. "What matters is no one will find you out here. There's no way to escape. No place to go if you do get free."

Juvens led the way, the rest of us falling meekly into line behind him. But I stopped several feet short of the doorway, my spirit rebelling. I couldn't go in there. Couldn't be confined. Once inside, we might never get back out. What had started out as an exciting vacation had turned into a nightmare. Could things get any worse? I was afraid I knew the answer to that question.

The kidnapper stepped close, pointing his gun directly at me. "Move."

My feet wouldn't budge. Stepping closer, he prodded me hard in the back with the gun barrel. The fear and rage in me came out in a scream worthy of a horror movie.

Chapter Eight

I scrambled ahead, stopping right inside the door. There would be a bruise where the kidnapper had shoved his gun into my back. "The house doesn't look safe."

He scowled. "Safe enough. It has stood through earthquakes and hurricanes."

"Can you at least free our hands?" I asked, hoping once my hands were free I'd feel some sense of hope or relief.

The kidnapper glared at me. "When you are locked in the room, but not now."

Walking further into the house, I glanced around at our prison. Everything visible appeared to be made of marble or varnished wood, but there were cracks in the floor, and the whole house seemed to lean. A statue I recognized as Mary, the mother of Jesus, was lying smashed on the floor. Looking up, I saw the ceiling had a large crack.

A spiral polished wooden staircase, once beautiful, now suffered a broken handrail and several missing steps. Other steps were warped, cracked, or splintered. The kidnapper motioned with his gun. "Up the stairs."

I studied them skeptically. Were they sturdy enough to hold us? Chad, standing beside me, clenched his jaw and stepped forward. "I'll go first."

He carefully stepped onto the first step, then proceeded to the second and the third. Pausing where the fourth step should have been, he stretched a leg to put his foot carefully on the next stair, but with his hands bound, there was no way to steady himself.

Overbalancing, Chad tried to throw his weight forward to skip over the missing step. Instead, he fell sideways, crashing into what was left of the rail. The sound of breaking wood filled the air as the rail splintered, and Chad tumbled to the floor.

My breath caught. What if he'd been at the top of the stairs when he fell instead of the bottom? What if he fell again? If Chad with all his athletic ability couldn't make it up the stairs, there was no way the rest of us would be able to.

The kidnapper must have been thinking the same thing because he pulled out a pocket knife and sliced the tape binding my hands. My left hand stung. Glancing down, I saw blood. He'd nicked me with the knife, and I wasn't so sure it was an accident. Was this his way of paying me back for the kick I'd landed?

He freed the others, and we all trudged up the stairs, avoiding the empty spots where stairs were cracked or missing altogether. When we reached the top, we were forced to climb yet another set of stairs which opened onto a hallway. The floor looked like marble embedded with pieces of different colored stones, creating a mosaic design.

The kidnapper opened the door and gestured for Juvens to enter. Once our driver was inside, the man shut the door and slid a bolt into place.

He opened a second door and motioned for us to enter. Chad stepped aside for me to go first, putting himself between me and the kidnapper. I took a tentative step forward and stopped. Uncomfortable heat and dizziness filled me. I couldn't get enough air. I had to calm down. I made myself count slowly, inhaling through my nose and exhaling through my mouth until I was breathing normally again. Panic wouldn't help.

"In the room!" the kidnapper ordered.

When I hesitated, he shoved me, and I stumbled. With a cry,

I put my hands out to catch myself, but landed hard on my knees. A stale, mildew smell assaulted my nose. The others hurried in behind me, prodded by the kidnapper.

"Ewww," Jen said. "You expect us to stay in here? There's mold everywhere, and could the walls be any dustier?"

For once I agreed with her.

The room had probably been a bedroom but was now totally empty of furniture. Bars covered the only two windows. A large diagonal crack divided the glass pane on one window, while the other had part of the pane missing. At least we would have a little fresh air.

"We'll be okay," Chad said. "Do what he says."

Jen turned to face him. "We'll be okay? Really? Because I'm not seeing it."

Chad gave a slight nod. "Me either. But my trust is in God, and he is greater than these men."

Jen rolled her eyes. "So now we're going to get religious and hope God rescues us?"

"It's not like that," Chad replied.

"All of you shut up," the kidnapper said. Turning, he said something in Creole to his nephew, who had entered the room behind him. The nephew left, then returned with a small pile of blankets, which he tossed to the floor. He left again and returned with four bottles of water and a loaf of bread.

"You have blankets, water, and food. The toilet is here," the kidnapper said as he pulled open a door. We were looking at a bucket in a closet.

"You have got to be kidding!" Jen said. "You expect us to use a bucket as a toilet?"

"You don't have to, but it would be better if you do. Enough talk. I am leaving now."

The kidnapper turned and walked out the door, his nephew following.

"Wait," Chad said. "What about Juvens? Did you give him food and water too?"

"Not your worry," the man growled as he shut the door. The metallic click of a bolt sliding into place sounded like a shot in the otherwise silent room.

Chapter Nine

Jen stamped her foot. "They can't do this!"

"They just did, so obviously they can!" The words exploded from my mouth with a mind of their own. I spun on my heel, walked over to the window, and peered out. It was a long way down. The sight alone made me lightheaded.

Levi tapped my shoulder. "It's my fault. I wanted to go to the mission."

I shook my head. "It's not your fault. I don't know how that man knew we were going to be at the mission, but if he hadn't kidnapped us there, he would have gotten us at the resort. He was obviously determined to get us ever since I foiled his robbery."

Even as I reassured Levi, questions filled my mind. How long had this been planned? Did the kidnapper know that Dr. M would be visiting the clinic this week, bringing drugs with him? I voiced the questions to no one in general.

"I don't know the answers to those questions," Chad replied. "And it's not your fault any more than Levi's. If you hadn't stopped the theft, there would be a lot of patients without the medicines they need. And you don't know he wouldn't decide double money is better than a single payout. The bigger question now is how we're going to escape."

"Escape? And do what?" Jen asked.

"Go back to the resort. Or the clinic. Find Dad and Mom," he said.

"How are we going to do that? Even if we get away, we're

miles from anywhere and they have our phones. They have all our stuff." Jen scowled.

"We can't stay here," Chad said. "And not only because I don't want Dad to have to pay out money. Normally a kidnapper will release the victim if he receives the money. At least that's the way it is here. Kidnapping is almost a career opportunity. But from what the guy said, it sounds like this might be more personal than a random kidnapping. If he has something against Mom and Dad or the clinic, then he may not let us go even if he gets the money."

My heart plummeted. This wasn't what I wanted to hear. I spoke up. "I agree with Chad. I wouldn't trust him to let us go even if he did get the money."

I began pacing back and forth, one end of the room to the other. Levi shifted so he was facing me. His eyes met mine. I stopped "What, Levi?"

Jen turned and stared at my twin. His lips parted, but the words were stuck. This happened when he felt uncomfortable or under pressure. He hadn't had trouble speaking since joining the Michaels family, but it was no wonder the problem was recurring.

Jen huffed. "Honestly. We're in big trouble here, and he won't even talk?"

I glared at her. "He won't—he can't—talk to us because he knows how you feel about us. He can sense your disapproval even without the condescending way you act toward us."

Her eyes grew wide. "You mean it's my fault he can't talk? Well, how convenient to have me to blame! But you hardly know me. Did you forget you were adopted out of foster care less than a year ago?"

"How could I forget with you acting like we are still foster kids? And you can just—"

Chad's eyes narrowed. "Enough! If we want to get out of this alive, we need to work together. We're all family now no matter how we joined. Remember, Jen, I was adopted out of foster care too. We have nothing to be ashamed of. No one gets to pick the parents they are born to. You didn't get to choose to have rich parents while Lexi, Levi, and I got birth parents who didn't take care of us. Besides, just think …we're all adopted into God's family, and at least he knows where we're at."

"And there's the religion again!" Jen said.

Chad frowned. "Doesn't your family go to church?"

Jen shrugged. "Well, yeah. On Sundays, but we don't talk about religion during the week like Uncle David and Aunt Maggie. You'd never find my dad volunteering at a Christian clinic in a third-world country."

I faced Chad. "That's what doesn't make sense about this whole God thing. God could have kept this from happening. Your parents are good people. He should have kept the kidnapping from happening."

"Yes, but he didn't, so we need to figure out what to do. He gave us brains to use. Besides, while God might not have kept this from happening, he'll go through it with us."

A look of resolve filled Levi's face. He reached into his pocket, pulled out the knife he'd bought as a souvenir, and handed it to Chad. So now I knew what he wanted to say! He still has his knife"

"Wow, smart, Levi! Guess they should have thought of searching your pockets!" Chad pulled open each attachment. "Besides the knife, we have a screwdriver, pliers, and wire cutters all in one."

Jen frowned. "What good will it be? Are we going to saw through the metal bars, then jump three stories down or tie blankets together for a rope?"

My temper started to flare. "We have to try. Chad could run out of insulin. Or the men could leave us here and not return.

Then we'd really be in trouble."

Jen opened, then closed her mouth. I ignored her and turned to Chad. "Do you have any ideas?" Desperation was seeping into my spirit as the reality of our situation became clearer.

"Not yet." Pocketing the knife, he walked over to the window and yanked on the bars. Nothing happened. He yanked again.

If I'd hoped for an easy way out, the hope died with Chad's failure to remove the bars. My desperation grew tangled with the anger welling inside me. I stepped forward, grabbed the bars myself, and started yanking. I gripped harder, my arms and shoulders starting to ache as I yanked on the bars, all the while knowing there was no way I could go out the window even if the bars came loose.

I sank to the floor, my energy spent.

Chapter Ten

Chad dropped to the floor beside me. "It'll be okay. We can think this through and come up with a solution."

Jen sighed dramatically. Ignoring her, Chad walked over and looked out the window.

I got off the floor and stood by him. The sun was setting. I felt like we'd left for the mission days ago, though only a few hours had passed. The sun was painting the sky red and orange over the vast wilderness outside. A loneliness, so deep it reached my toes, consumed me. I blinked rapidly, determined not to fall into despair, but my heart ached as never before. Longing for home filled me.

I dropped back to the floor and pulled one of the blankets around me. I wasn't cold, just chilled. I watched as Chad paced back and forth. Finally, he sat near me. Jen and Levi joined us. I scooted closer to Levi, hoping his nearness would ease the ache within. After all, other than the brief time we were separated when he was in the boys' home, he had been the one constant in my life.

Chad finally spoke up. "Obviously there are two ways out of this room—the windows or the door."

Jen interrupted. "Except the windows are three stories up and have bars, and the door is deadbolted from the outside."

Levi began rolling and unrolling the bottom of his sweatshirt. I tapped his hand. He pulled his knees to his chest and locked his arms around them. Jen turned to look at him.

"Leave him alone," I spat out before she had a chance to say a word. "We all have our own ways of dealing with stress."

I turned and focused on Chad but didn't miss Jen's mouth dropping open in reaction to my outburst. I felt heat creep up my neck. She hadn't actually said anything negative about Levi. I'd merely assumed she was going to.

Chad spoke up. "As Jen pointed out, the windows are barred, and the door is secured from the outside. Even if we got the bars off, we are too high to jump or drop. But as Jen said, we could make a rope from these blankets."

"I wasn't suggesting anything," Jen protested.

I shuddered, wondering if I could force myself out the window even to save my own life. Levi linked his little finger through mine and squeezed. I squeezed back.

Chad continued, "But the bars are secured by heavy bolts, so it might be easier to get out the door."

Jen tilted her head. "Easier to get out the door?"

Chad nodded. "They have to come back to check on us. There are two of them and four of us."

"But the two of them have guns," Jen pointed out.

"We'd have to catch them by surprise," Chad said.

He had my interest. "How?"

Chad glanced around the room. "The door opens inward. Maybe two of us could position ourselves behind the door. When the door opens and they step in, we could jump them from behind."

Jen snorted. "The four of us take down two full-grown men with guns?"

"I'd be willing to try," I said. "I learned techniques in the classes Dr. M had me take."

Jen stared at me and shook her head. "Really? You're going to tackle one of them?"

I ignored her.

Chad grinned. "She did stop the kidnapper from taking the

drugs. It might work, but I wish we had Juvens with us. He's heavier than I am, so we'd have serious weight to tackle the other two. One way or another, we'll need to free him once we get out."

I nodded. "I think we are going to have to create a diversion to draw the kidnappers into the room and keep them from noticing two of us are out of sight."

Chad turned to Jen. "You could be lying on the floor groaning and clutching your stomach. They might hurry over to check on you."

"Like they'd even care," Jen replied. "It sounds like a bad movie plot to me."

"You have a better idea?" Chad asked.

Jen hesitated, then shook her head. "Okay then, let's try to sleep. We'll rest up and wait for our chance."

Chapter Eleven

A soft thud woke me. Light shone through the window, letting me know it was morning. I tried to sit up, but my body ached from sleeping on the floor and all the bumps yesterday. I grimaced as I slowly stretched out my arms, then pushed myself into a sitting position. I looked around, trying to identify the sound that had woken me. Chad was doing squat thrusts in the corner of the room. I rubbed the sleep from my eyes and yawned.

Chad looked my way. "Morning."

"What are you doing?" I asked.

"Exercising like I do every morning. Thought I'd keep my routine." Chad did three more fast squat thrusts complete with push-ups.

"How can you be so calm?"

"What I said about God knowing our situation is true. I have to hold onto that. Have hope."

"Dr. M told me something from the Bible about hope—something about God having a plan for our lives—for hope or something. I forget."

Chad sat next to me. "Oh, the verse is in Jeremiah. God gives us a future and a hope—Dad's favorite verse."

"He has a favorite part of the Bible?"

"Sure. My favorite verse is about hope too—in Romans. Do you want to hear it?"

I stopped and turned to him. "You memorized it?"

Chad grinned. "Memorizing is what you do with Scripture.

You read it. You memorize it. You think about it."

"I thought that was for adults or preachers."

"Nope. I guess I don't talk about the Bible at home as much as I should, but here's my verse. 'I pray that God, the source of hope, will fill you completely with joy and peace because you trust in him. Then you will overflow with confident hope through the power of the Holy Spirit.'"

"You understand all those words?"

"Sure. God is the source of hope, and if we trust him, he gives us joy and peace. Then we'll overflow with confident hope. I especially like that—confident hope. It makes me feel strong even when I'm not."

I looked at him. "I'm not sure I know what confident hope is."

"It's the kind of hope God gives— a hope that starts with trusting him. And when you trust him with your life, your salvation, your future, he gives you peace and joy. Then hope is a way of life for you."

"Well, hope has sure never been a way of life for me or Levi. We've never known hope or peace."

"I think you didn't dare have hope before. You were in the system too long and moved too many times to have hope. But those days are over." He grinned. "Now we are stuck with you, and you are stuck with us. No matter what happens."

"What if we don't get out of here? Get back to Dr. and Mrs. M?"

"Then we know God had a different plan. We may not like or understand his plan, but that's where the trust comes in. And if we trust him, then we'll have the peace and joy and—well, the ability to have confident hope no matter what happens."

Chad hopped up and resumed his exercises with renewed vigor. I watched him. He certainly seemed to know what he was talking about. I'd never met anyone with as much confidence as my new big brother. And hope, whether it really was as justified as he seemed to believe.

Jen sat up sleepily. "Oh goodness. What now?"

"Chad exercising," I said.

Jen rolled her eyes before shutting them again, ignoring us.

Levi sat up. I knew he'd been listening to Chad talk about hope even though he'd pretended to be asleep. His face gave him away. We'd been attending church with the Michaels since we'd moved in with them, but the worship service had never been personal to me. Mostly I let my mind wander while the preacher talked. I didn't know how Levi felt because we'd never talked about God.

Chad stood, walked to the window, and looked out. "It's a long drop to the ground. I've measured out what we can do even cutting up our blankets, and I think we're going to have to go with our plan to exit through the door."

"Oh great," Jen said, eyes still closed. "I'll knock on the door and ask to be let out."

The sound of a car arriving ended the discussion. We all stood, straining to hear anything that might give us a clue of what was going to happen next. The gate squeaked open. Then footsteps sounded downstairs. Slowly they ascended the stairs.

"Are we going to jump them?" I whispered, ready for whatever would happen next. Levi stood beside me.

Chad shook his head. "We're not ready."

The steps stopped outside our door. The bolt slid back, and the door swung open. The younger kidnapper, Stevens, stood holding another loaf of bread and four water bottles. I hadn't noticed the dryness in my mouth until then. I stepped forward and eagerly reached for one of the bottles.

Stevens looked at me. Holding my gaze, he dropped three of the water bottles and the bread. After twisting the lid off, he tipped up the fourth bottle, and drank. He handed the bottle to me with barely a sip left, wiped his mouth with his hand, and smirked.

Heat rushed through me. I wanted to knock the smug look right off his face.

Then he spoke in accented English. "We wait to hear if parents get money. We get money, you go. No money ..." Stevens pulled his finger across his throat. Then he turned and left, locking the deadbolt behind him. I looked at the water bottle in disgust and dropped it. I turned to Chad. "How does 'sending the money' work?"

Chad shrugged. "Dunno. Never been kidnapped before."

Laughter threatened to spill out, not because the situation was humorous, but because I was so tense. Chad's casual tone was kind of funny —like this was an everyday event. A nervous giggle broke free.

Jen stared at me. "What's so funny?"

"Nothing, but if I don't laugh, I'm going to fall apart. And that won't help anything."

Jen looked at me for a few seconds, then scowled. "Well, I'm thirsty." She picked up one of the bottles and drank.

Chad picked up another and handed it to me. "You drink half of this."

I shook my head. "You need it worse. You can't risk dehydrating."

"We'll share," Chad insisted.

Levi held out his bottle also. I accepted and took a drink. We were used to sharing what we had, sometimes in order to survive a bad situation.

"Oh, and I'm the bad one because I'm drinking my own." Jen put the lid on then slammed her bottle down.

"No one said anything," Chad said. "Levi and I chose to share ours. No big deal."

"Of course not," Jen said, sarcasm tinting her words.

Chad faced her. "Look. Things are probably going to get a lot worse before they get better. The only way we are going to get out of here and home safely is if we all get over ourselves and work together."

Jen rolled her eyes. "Whatever."

Chad was right, and I knew I could have a better attitude. Still, Jen didn't have to be such a snob. There was a group of girls like her at school, and I made a point to avoid them. But Chad was doing his best to get us to work together, so I bit back the words I wanted to say and nodded in agreement.

"Let's be ready to go out the door next time it opens," he said.

Chapter Twelve

Chad's words started a torrent of anxiety flooding through me, but Jen crossed her arms and stared at him. "Well, I hope you have a better plan than jumping the bad guys and going out the door because I am not going to spend all day in this room eating bread, drinking water, and ... and using a bucket in the closet."

"Hope you have a bladder the size of Texas then," Chad replied, "because this is the way it is for now."

Jen's lower lip dropped into a pout. "Well, excuse me for wanting to be civilized!"

I bit back a grin.

Chad crossed his arms, a serious look on his face.

"What?" I asked.

"All this tension and girl-drama isn't going to get us anywhere."

Jen's mouth dropped open. "Did you say girl-drama? Really?"

Chad put his hands up in mock surrender. "Whatever is going on between you two, we need to get past all the differences and work together or ..."

Before Chad could finish his sentence, a jolt sent me toppling into him. I regained my balance and started to ask what had happened, when the house started to rock. A crash of metal and glass sounded below, causing Jen and me to scream in unison. I tried to stay balanced, but I couldn't. A stronger jolt shook the entire house, and we all toppled to the floor while plaster rained down on us.

The rolling stopped. Chad picked himself up from the floor. "Earthquake! Has to be!"

"I've never been in an earthquake," I said, hating the way my voice trembled.

Chad shook his head. "Me either."

Levi sat on the floor and wrapped his arms around his knees. Jen brushed plaster from her face. "Is it over?"

Chad had no sooner shrugged when another forceful jolt shook the building. The wall I'd been leaning on split, forming a large crack. I shrieked as I scurried to the other side of the room. The window was still secure, but now there was an opening in the wall.

"The house is falling!" Jen screamed. "We're going to be killed!"

"Out that way," Chad said, pointing to the door. Like the window, the door remained standing, but the wall showed extensive cracks, including one letting in daylight along the doorjamb.

Chad kicked at the door jamb, and the entire wooden frame fell forward into the hall. I climbed out after him, then froze at the sight in front of me. The stairs had been torn from the wall. A few steps forward and we'd plunge straight down. I scampered back, my breathing ragged.

Loud voices reached us from below. The kidnappers! We stood unmoving, out of sight of anyone who might be in the stairwell below. My peripheral vision caught Jen and Levi scrambling over the fallen door to join us as I asked Chad in a whisper, "What are they saying?"

"I can't understand everything," he whispered back. "They are disagreeing over whether to stay or not. The nephew wants to take us, but the kidnapper says he's not going near those stairs and not to worry, we have no way out. He's insisting on getting away from the house in case it falls."

"And he doesn't care if we die in here? I don't think our parents would pay if we were all dead," I said.

"The kidnappers are more worried about themselves right now," Chad said.

The voices dwindled into the distance. Then we heard a door open and close. I was about to ask how we were going to get out when a loud sound drew my attention upward. The ceiling had fractured, showering us with large chunks of plaster and cement.

Simultaneously, a crack like thunder came from under us. I put my hands over my ears and screamed. This was the end!

Chapter Thirteen

A hard grip dug into my shoulders. "Lexi, stop!" The hands shook me slightly. "Stop!"

I did.

And opened my eyes.

Chad was inches from me, holding my shoulders firmly. "Losing control isn't going to help. We have to get out of here."

"How?" My voice trembled. "I don't want to be trapped here if the house falls, but there's no way out."

"We'll have to go out over the rail," Chad said. "The stairs are no good anymore."

Jen's face was white; her eyes wide as she stared around. I glanced around too. A film of panic enveloped me. Where was Levi?

"Levi?" I called frantically. "Levi? Where are you?"

A soft bird call sounded behind me. Levi was sitting on the floor, making bird whistles while he sliced at his blanket with the knife he'd purchased at the mission. I tapped his hand to stop him, but he shook his head and held up the strip of blanket he had sliced away.

Chad looked at Levi, then back at the place where the steps had once been. "Levi has the right idea. I guess we need the blanket ropes after all. But first we need to free Juvens."

Chad headed toward the closest room to the stairs where we'd seen our captors shove Juvens inside. He quickly returned, looking perplexed. "The door was unlocked, and the room's empty."

"So he was able to escape!" I said. "Then why didn't he come to check on us?"

Chad shrugged. "Maybe they took him somewhere else."

"Or maybe they killed him if they weren't going to get a ransom for him!" Jen suggested.

"Don't even think that!" Chad answered sharply. "Let's hope he got away alive and safe."

Sitting next to Levi, Chad began knotting together the blanket strips Levi had cut. "Get the other blankets. We'll need more than this. And hurry! There could be more aftershocks, and we want to be out of here."

"The first tremor in 2010 was followed by two more tremors on the same day. Then there was another one ten days later," Levi said, as he handed Chad another strip.

That wasn't what I wanted to hear. My hands shook as I ducked back into the room where we'd been held and grabbed up the blankets from the floor. I shook off the plaster and other debris before scrambling back out to hand them to Chad.

By now Levi was only making an initial cut with his knife, while Chad's strong hand finished ripping the strips away. I grabbed two and started knotting. Jen did the same. With all of us working together, the four blankets became one long rope in just a few minutes.

Getting to his feet, Chad looked around for some place to anchor the rope. The remaining railing of the stairwell was obviously too wobbly. But a small, barred window, the glass pane now shattered, looked out at the top of the landing where the staircase opened onto the third-floor corridor.

Knocking out the remaining glass, Chad secured one end of the blanket rope with strong knots to the window bars. Then he wrapped the rope around his wrist and tugged hard. The blanket rope held fast. Tossing the end of the rope down into the stairwell, he turned to look at us.

"Okay, let's get out of here. I'll go first since I'm the heaviest. If I get down safely, you three shouldn't have any difficulty."

"Are we supposed to feel better?" Jen demanded. "What if it breaks? Then you'll fall, and we'll be stuck up here!"

Despite her final self-serving statement, she actually looked concerned for Chad, her face pale. Maybe she really did care about someone other than herself.

Chad shrugged. "We've got no choice. I'll take my chances."

With the rope still wrapped around his wrist, Chad lowered himself over the edge of the landing until he was swinging freely over the empty space of the stairwell. Peering gingerly over the edge, I could see the second-floor landing, remnants of the staircase still attached.

Chad slid down the rope far enough to balance his feet briefly on the crumbled remnants of the second-floor landing below, moving his hands from one knot to the next as he went. Then he pushed out again. I braced myself for the rope to tear and drop Chad to the ground floor below. But it held and, moments later, Chad was at the bottom of the stairwell.

Jen gasped. "Is he related to Spiderman or something?"

Looking up at us, Chad called out, "Lexi, you're next. Grab the rope with both hands as close to the top as you can, then lower yourself backwards over the edge and slide down one knot at a time, using the knots to steady your feet. I'm sure you've done this in gym class. This is no different."

I looked down at Chad and tried to take a breath, but the air refused to fill my lungs. "I can't. I couldn't in gym class. I can't now. The rest of you go on and send help back for me."

"Yes, you can," Chad insisted. "And you need to do it right now because who knows when another tremor might hit. Or the kidnappers decide to come back."

Merely looking down into the stairwell with a broken and twisted staircase was making me dizzy. "I really, really can't!"

"Oh, get out of the way!" Jen said impatiently. "I never had any problem with the rope climb at school. You'd better be ready to catch me, Chad, if I let go!"

I didn't feel better seeing Jen scrambling down with minimal effort, her sandals seeking out one knot after another until Chad caught her and helped her down the last few feet.

"Come on!" she called up to me. "Don't be such a wimp. You're putting everyone else in danger!"

I looked at Levi.

"You can do this," he said. Hauling the length of knotted blankets back toward us, he wrapped my two hands around the rope above a knot, then pushed me gently toward the open space. I didn't resist any further, though I was shaking with terror, especially once I lost the safety of a floor and found myself dangling out over empty space, with only my white-knuckled grip between me and the ground far below.

"You can do it!" Chad called up. "Shut your eyes and don't look down. Come on! Jen and I are here to catch you!"

Squeezing my eyes tight shut, I tried to imitate what Chad had done. But I could not hold my body weight nor get my feet braced against the knots. The rough blanket material ripped at the skin on my hands as I slid helplessly down the rope.

"Slow down!" Chad called. "Use the knots!"

"Yeah, if I can, you can!" Jen chimed in. "Don't be such a baby!"

Jen was more helpful than she knew because at her words, my fear gave way to anger, fueling my resolve. I'd show her! This wasn't going to be one more way for my spoiled-brat new cousin to display her superiority!

I had just managed to steady my sneakers against the second-floor landing when another tremor shook the house. The sound of crashing glass and splintering wood filled the air. A sharp pain seared my temple, and I could feel a trickle of what had to be blood running down my cheek.

Then the tremor stopped, and I discovered I was still holding on. Eyes closed, I let the rope slide between my hands until they came to another knot, then loosened my feet and slid them downwards until they came up hard against another knot. My legs felt weak, and I started to shake, but I repeated the motions again, then again. Just like gym! You can do this!

An eternity later—at least what seemed so—I felt hands grabbing me. Then there was solid ground under my feet. Letting go of the rope, I opened my eyes. Grinning down at me, Chad gave me an approving pat on the shoulder. "Good job, though you've got a nasty cut there on the side of your face."

I swiped at my face, and my hand came away bloody. But there was no time to worry about a few cuts and bruises. Where was Levi? Had the last tremor done more structural damage?

"Levi!" I called out. "Are you okay up there?"

High above, my twin's rusty-hued head thrust itself over the edge of the stairwell. Then he grabbed for the blanket rope and swung neatly into space.

"You're hurt!" he said as soon as he touched down beside me.

I'd forgotten about the cut, but now realized blood was dripping off my chin onto my shirt. With no further commentary, Levi once again dug out his knife from his pocket. He sliced a length of blanket off the end of the rope and handed it to me. As he did so, Chad yanked on the rope as hard as he could.

"What are you doing?" I asked, pressing the blanket material to the cut on my cheek.

"Trying to get the rope. If the kidnappers see it, they'll know we've escaped. Besides, it might come in handy later. You never know."

Dropping my makeshift compress, I joined the others,

putting our combined weight into pulling on the rope, but it broke off in the middle rather than the top.

"Better than nothing," Chad said, coiling the rope around his waist and tying it off with a flourish.

My cut seemed to have stopped bleeding, so I didn't bother recovering the piece of blanket before following Chad over chunks of staircase and other debris to the front door. We waited while Chad eased the door open and cautiously looked outside.

"I don't see anyone. The black car we saw when we got here is gone, so they must have driven off. I do see the van, though it's not very drivable!"

Stepping up to peer around him, I saw chunks of brick, marble, and wood had landed on the van, breaking the windshield and smashing the hood and roof. "Do you think our backpacks might still be in there?"

"Let's find out." Chad led the way to the van. Wrestling open the rear door, he climbed into the luggage compartment.

As he did so, I glanced back at the house. From this distance, the amount of damage was evident. Part of the roof had caved in, and wide cracks ran up the walls all the way to the third story. Just then a low rumble signaled the collapse of the front porch, followed by an avalanche as the front wall gave way. We'd been lucky to make it out alive!

"Yes!" Chad exclaimed triumphantly from inside the van. He emerged holding a backpack. "They're all still here!"

He handed the packs out one at a time. I peered into mine. The rest of my money was gone as was my remaining bottle of water, but my iPad and phone were still in the concealed waterproof pouch. Relief flooded through me.

Chad was rifling through his own backpack. "Everything is here except my money. I guess that was to be expected, but at least I've still got my insulin. Oh, and they took my water too.

Any of you got water?"

As Levi and Jen both shook their heads, I spoke up, "Mine's gone too. Now we know where they got what they brought us to drink—from our own backpacks. We're going to have a problem if we have to walk very far."

"I don't care about the water as much as my money!" Jen complained loudly. "Which was a whole lot more than yours so a whole lot worse! I'll bet the nephew ripped us off. He was already digging through our wallets when he made us give him our things!"

"Money can be replaced!" I said flatly. "What matters is getting out of here. And if we don't have water, then we'd really better get a move on. If the van isn't smashed too bad, maybe we can drive back to the resort."

"Maybe—if it still runs and we had the keys," Chad said. "Any of you know how to hotwire a car?"

We didn't have time to even try. The sound of a car engine made us all jump. Whirling around, I saw a black car heading up the lane toward the property gate, which was standing open. The car looked to be the same one we'd seen parked when we arrived. If our kidnappers had used it to flee, they clearly hadn't gone far.

A shout rang out as the driver suddenly gunned the engine and accelerated. Stepping away from the van, I caught sight of the scarred man behind the steering wheel. His nephew was leaning out the passenger window, shouting something in Creole. Even from this distance, we could easily read the anger on their faces.

"Run!" Chad yelled.

Chapter Fourteen

Chad took off running through the overgrown garden, jumping with fluid motion over the debris and fallen trees in his way. No wonder he excelled in every sport he played. I ran more slowly. Jen and Levi were behind me. A glance back showed the black car slamming to a stop beside the van and our kidnappers jumping out.

I lengthened my stride as Jen raced past me, and Levi fell in place beside me. Beyond the garden was an abandoned orchard, so overgrown that a glance back no longer revealed the kidnappers as we zigzagged through tree trunks. I was already despairing. How were we to escape when the only opening we'd seen in the high metal fence surrounding the property was the gate behind us?

I was thankful I'd traded my flip-flops for sneakers before leaving the resort, but I still felt clumsy as I attempted to jump over the debris without slowing. My side cramped, and I wanted to stop running, but the shouts of the kidnappers told me they were quickly gaining on us. And now I could see the black metallic glint of the perimeter fence. As I'd expected, we were trapped!

Then a miracle happened—or at least it seemed so to me. Ahead, Chad and Jen disappeared under the sprawled branches of a huge tree, felled by the earthquake. As I scrambled behind them, my leg scraped against the bark and ragged edge of a broken limb. I didn't mind the pain when I saw the tree had fallen across the perimeter fence, so this section was flattened by the weight of the tree.

I heard Levi's quickened breathing behind me as I ducked and scrambled after Chad and Jen. Perhaps the kidnappers hadn't seen where we'd disappeared. For the first time, their shouts sounded further away.

We emerged on the other side of the fence into dense forest. Our speed was hindered, but we had more cover. As I raced forward, a large hand suddenly closed around my wrist. I bit back a scream as I realized Chad, not a kidnapper, was grabbing me.

"Watch out!" Holding my wrist firmly, Chad put his other arm out to stop Levi. My mouth dropped open as I looked down. In my panic, I hadn't been paying attention to what was right in front of me. Just inches from the toes of my sneakers, the forest floor had split open in a long crack at least three feet wide. I'd have plunged headlong into it if Chad hadn't stopped me!

The sounds of pounding feet alerted us that the kidnappers were still in pursuit.

"I've got an idea!" Chad whispered urgently. "Follow me, and no noise! Try not to break any branches."

Dropping to a crouch, he scrambled under a patch of thick underbrush to the left. I followed at his heels as he dropped to a belly-crawl a few meters in to worm his way into even denser foliage. A glance back confirmed Levi and Jen were right behind. We were hardly noiseless, but our pursuers' shouts as they crashed through the brush covered the noise we made.

As the shouts drew near, Chad whispered with even more urgency, "Nobody move or even breathe! With any luck, they'll think we jumped the ravine and kept going!"

I held my breath. Stretched out beside me, Levi was making no sound, but on my other side I could hear Jen loudly gasping air until I elbowed her sharply. The crashing and shouts were right on us. Surely they would see the marks where we'd ducked into hiding! But whether because the noise they made breaking and stomping the vegetation or they were moving too fast to look down, their noisy passage did not slow but carried our pursuers straight forward. A sharp, angry exclamation in Creole indicated they'd likely stumbled over the crevice, but within seconds they noisily moved off deeper into the forest.

I started to push myself to my knees, but Chad grabbed my arm. "We're not safe yet. When they don't find us, they'll likely circle back, so everyone keep quiet until we've found a place to hide. I've already got an idea of somewhere they won't look for us."

Signaling for the rest of us to follow, Chad belly-crawled further to the left through the underbrush. When he stopped, I saw—just beyond his head and shoulders—the clay-hued slit in the forest floor opened by the earthquake. Only here the slit was even wider—the closest trees were uprooted and tilted, some sprawling into the crevice, others with their roots sticking into the air like a nest of giant earthworms.

Beside me, Jen hissed, "Are you kidding? How are we going to get across that?"

"We're not. We're going in." Chad was peering into the crevice's depth. "It's not as far down as you think. Maybe a little more than my height. And this is one place they won't likely think we'd go. Trust me."

Chad chose a spot where a fallen tree had already collapsed the bank into a small avalanche of dirt, rocks, and vegetation to slide down into the crevice. This time I was last. Once at the bottom, I realized Chad was right. The edges of the crevice were far enough overhead so even if we stood up, we'd be invisible from the forest floor.

"Let's go. And we should grab branches to make sure we don't leave any footprints in case they do check down here."

We now understood what Chad had in mind and scrambled as quickly as we could along the bottom of the crevice. This time Chad insisted on bringing up the rear, using a leafy branch from one of the toppled trees to disturb any marks of our passing. The earth underfoot was loose and crumbling, making our progress slow, and soon the crevice started to narrow again. But before we were forced to climb out, we came to another uprooted tree. The tree had tipped forward toward the crevice so the trunk and branches provided a semblance of ceiling for the full length of the fallen tree, with the roots marking the end of the crevice.

We waited for Chad, still brushing away our tracks, to catch up. "So, what now?" I asked.

I froze as a voice called out in Creole and another answered not more than a dozen paces away. By now I knew those voices, whether or not I knew what they were saying. The kidnappers had circled back and were now searching along the crevice.

Chad was already moving under the mass of branches and leaves at the top of the fallen tree, motioning frantically for us to follow. I crawled in after him, trying to keep my breathing and movements as quiet as possible. Once past the foliage, the tree trunk pressed in close overhead, making it as dark as a cave. The dirt was moist and damp beneath my hands as I crawled forward, and the darkness threatened to swallow me.

"Over here," Chad whispered.

I inched toward his voice, broken twigs and bark digging into my palms. I could hear Levi behind me, mumbling softly. When school started in the fall, the chemistry teacher was sure to be impressed at his memorization of the periodic table. As our kidnappers' voices floated closer, I reached back to touch his hand, a reminder of the need for silence. He immediately went quiet.

"Keep coming," Chad whispered.

I crawled until I hit up against Chad's legs in the dark. From what I could feel, he was sitting where the crevice came to an end. I leaned back against the earthen wall, not caring that dirt and twigs were dropping into my hair. Just a few feet away. I could hear Jen's annoyed muttering.

I reached out again for my twin's hand, linking my little finger with his. His breathing immediately calmed. Closing my eyes against the darkness, I forced myself to take a deep breath and blow it out to the count of ten, a relaxing technique our counselor had recommended. The seconds crawled by in silence.

Suddenly I tensed as the crashing and breaking of vegetation grew closer, then directly above us. Our younger captor said something in Creole, and the older one replied, his voice tinged with anger. After the exchange, they moved on. As silence once again reigned, I released the breath I hadn't realized I was holding.

I turned toward Chad and whispered, "Did you hear what they said?"

"Yes, they say we have vanished and must have somehow doubled back to the road leading out of here. They are going to look for us there."

"Then we can leave!" Jen whispered. "So why are we still sitting here?"

"For one, we need to be sure they're really gone," Chad explained. "Besides, this is as safe a place as any to wait until we can call Mom and Dad to let them know where we are and what's happened. They must have been frantic when we didn't make it home last night."

"And how do we do that?" Jen snapped. "Our phones didn't work at the mission. Why would they work now? Especially with the earthquake. If there are cell towers out here, they are probably down like the trees."

"We can at least try before we give up!" Chad had pulled his phone from his backpack. I could see him frown in its LED light as he studied the screen. "You are right, unfortunately. There's no service."

Reaching into my own pack, I pulled out my iPad and opened the flashlight app. Light flooded our shelter. Chad immediately reached over and turned the iPad over so the light burrowed into the ground. "If the kidnappers are still out there, they might see the light. We need to save the battery power for later." His suggestion was common sense. Even Jen didn't protest.

We had just finished powering down our phones and iPads and packing them back into our backpacks when a fresh tremor shook our shelter. Dirt poured down on us, and the massive log, our ceiling, shook and settled lower.

"Out!" Chad yelled.

He didn't need to repeat his command. I followed Levi back down the tunnel the tree trunk had made of our crevice and through the snarl of branches and leaves, with Jen and Chad close behind. Dirt, rocks, breaking twigs, and branches tumbled down on us. Even more frightening was the shaking of the earth below our feet and to either side. As we emerged into the light, I felt the movement of a tree toppling nearby, causing the sides of the crevice to crumble.

"Up, up! We've got to get out of here!" Chad wasn't even trying to whisper anymore as he led the scramble up the side of the ravine.

He didn't have to urge us. To my horror, the ground was cracking right down the center of the crevice. Even as Chad grabbed my hand and yanked me to firm ground, dirt and debris began spilling into the new slit in the earth. Then the tree trunk under which we'd sheltered crashed down to where we'd been sitting.

The tremor stopped, but we were now stranded on the bank and covered in dirt and debris. Jen stamped her foot. "Well, great! Just great!"

A nervous giggle escaped my lips as I took in the hat of twigs and leaves she was wearing. Jen spun to face me, hands on her hips.

"What is so funny?" she yelled. "You are constantly laughing when there is absolutely nothing to laugh about!"

"I ... I ... nothing." Another giggle burst free. "If you could see yourself!"

"You think you look any better?" Jen snapped as she began brushing at her hair and clothes.

"Yeah, but I'm used to it." I bit my bottom lip, struggling to get my giggles under control. I was sobered by a reminder our kidnappers could still be in earshot. I began shaking the dirt and vegetation from my own hair. Levi was already tidying himself.

Chad grinned. "Hey, better laugh than fall apart. We all look ridiculous, but at least we're alive. Time to make a plan." He paused, and his eyes clouded.

I faced him. "What's wrong?"

Chad forced a smile. "Nothing."

"Not hardly," I said. "Spill!"

"Well, I've been trying to ignore the issue, since we don't have any water. But I really need to hydrate. We all do, but for me, the situation is going to get ugly soon. We not only need to find water, but we'll need a way to strain and boil it."

Chad's admission caused my stomach to clench. Levi and I had been part of the Michaels family long enough to know how serious dehydration could be with Chad's diabetes. I spoke up. "Then I guess we'll have to find a house or building somewhere with running water—and a pot for boiling."

"I don't think we are anywhere near civilization," Chad

replied. "I sure didn't see any villages or buildings for a long time before we arrived here. We didn't cross any streams since the river near the mission either."

"Well, what about the house they were keeping us in?" I was grasping for any hint of hope. "Even if no one's living there, there still might be a water faucet or pump or well."

"Yeah, sure!" Jen put her hands on her hips and gave me a condescending look. "And run right back into the kidnappers! We'd still have to find a way to boil the water."

I faced her, copying her stance by putting my hands on my hips. "Well do you have a better idea? I'd love to hear."

I started to add more choice words but caught sight of Levi rolling and unrolling the bottom hem of his shirt. I touched his hand, then turned to Chad. "What do we do?"

Chad looked thoughtful. "Jen's right. We can't go back to the house since the kidnappers were headed there when we heard them last. They could even be calling in more of their gang to search for us. We've got to put distance between us and them while we have a chance. We'll have to hope we find water along the way—and a way to boil it— or pray for rain so we can collect water."

Jen scowled. "And if we don't find water?"

Chad's brows furrowed. "We will. If nothing else, we did cross the river between here and the mission, so if we head back down the mountain in the same general direction, we'll find water eventually. And there may be smaller streams or even pools of water."

I stifled a groan. "Let's get started then because I'm thirsty too. We also need to find a road back to the city. Which way is that from here?"

Jen stamped a foot. "How would we know? We could walk in circles for days until we die of thirst or starvation."

Levi tapped my hand. "Northwest."

"Northwest?" I asked.

Chad nodded. "He's right. The men took us straight south from the mission before we crossed the river, so the river is north of us."

"So, you're thinking we should head back to the mission?" I asked. "Do you even know the way from here?"

"Not the mission. If I'm right about the river we crossed, it runs west past the clinic. And the clinic is south of the mission, a whole lot closer to where we are. If we can head cross-country until we hit the river, we can follow it west to the clinic. Of course, if we get somewhere with cell service, we can call Mom and Dad to come get us."

"You make everything sound so easy!" Jen scowled. "Do you even know which way northwest is?"

Levi thrust his hands into his pockets. I could see him withdrawing, pulling into himself. I glared at Jen. "Levi has a compass, given to him by Dr. M on our birthday, and he's worn it fastened to his belt loop ever since. Remember, he had to take off the compass to go through security."

Jen rolled her eyes. "We all remember him going through security. I thought he was going to have a tantrum."

I opened my mouth to retort, but Chad gave both Jen and me a stern look. Then he turned to Levi. "Okay, Levi, you lead the way."

Chapter Fifteen

Step. Step. Step. I kept a rhythm going in my head, not sure I could take another step if I stopped. Everywhere I looked, there was devastation. Dirt had broken free; rocks had cascaded; trees had fallen.

This made walking slow, each stride taken with care. One wrong step and we could end up dislodging an avalanche of earth or stepping on a boulder that gave way underfoot. Sweat trickled down my face, the heat sweltering. If only it would rain to cool us down, but a deluge might dislodge more earth.

We couldn't have been walking more than an hour—no, not walking —climbing up and down the mountainside. Already my calves burned from the muscle strain. I bit at my bottom lip, not wanting to be the first to show pain. Mountain climbing was definitely not for me!

Finally, I broke the silence. "Am I the only one whose legs are cramping already?"

Jen swiped at the sweat, making pale streaks through the dirt on her face. "At least you're in shoes. I'm wearing these stupid sandals. I didn't know I needed hiking boots for this trip. Next time Dad and Mom go on a vacation without me, I'm staying home or with a friend."

"No one could have predicted this would happen," Chad said. Turning to me he added, "And this isn't your typical mountain climb. The shock waves have displaced a lot of earth. If we were on the other side of the river, we'd soon be to a town. There are towns over there, but there's not much on this side.

Taking the road would help, but of course, that's where the kidnappers are looking for us. Hopefully, we'll come across a path sooner or later."

We continued our scramble, sometimes downhill, sometimes up, so I knew we had to be making progress. Levi seemed satisfied we were on the right compass heading, but forest and underbrush all looked the same, like we were going around in circles. How many hours would it take to reach the river?

I was ready to rebel and demand a rest stop when Chad stumbled in front of me. As he went down on one knee, I grabbed his arm to help steady him. "Chad! Are you okay?"

Jen huffed. "Of course he's not okay."

Pushing himself back to his feet, Chad grimaced. "A bit drained from all this."

If Chad was feeling drained, what hope did the rest of us have? He seldom showed any sign of fatigue, not when he regularly ran half-marathons.

"Do you think your blood sugar is okay?" I asked.

"I have insulin in my pump and good batteries, but lack of water is the problem. If we can find the river or another source of water soon, I'll be okay. A good meal wouldn't hurt either."

We all agreed, but neither water nor a good meal appeared to be in our near future. We slowed our pace even further as the terrain became more challenging, requiring us to climb constantly over rocks and fallen trees. Glancing toward Chad, I saw his tightened mouth, his caramel-colored skin paler than usual. A weight like a rock settled in my stomach.

"Let's stop and rest," I suggested.

Chad clenched his jaw. "I can keep going."

I sat on a downed tree. "A few minutes rest won't matter. In fact, we'll probably move faster afterward."

"I want to keep going." A stubborn desperation filled Chad's voice.

I knew arguing was useless. Resigned, I stood. "Okay. Onward we go!"

Concern filled Levi's face. He looked toward me, a question in his eye. I nodded, and he checked his compass, then began leading the way. A new confidence seemed to fill him as he took the role of guide. Soon we were on a different terrain as the ground leveled, and a carpet of green grass stretched in front of us. I had a strong urge to lay on the soft grass and sleep, but I followed the others.

"Look!" Levi cried out. "Buildings!"

It was actually only one building—a small wooden structure beyond the field in a grove of trees.

"It must be a farm. Maybe we can find people ... and water."

As we drew closer, we could see the wooden structure, broken down with large gaps open to the weather. My legs had welcomed the break as we crossed the green flatland, but now the knot in my stomach tightened. If there were no people here, what was the likelihood we'd find water? We certainly hadn't seen any sign of a stream.

Chad quickened his pace. He was breathing hard, so I urged, "Slow down, Chad. Save your strength."

He only walked faster. "I don't want to slow down. Not when I'm seeing what might save our lives. Come on!"

He had shifted direction to head toward what looked like a grove of tall palm trees to the right of the broken-down shack. Only when we got close did I see the long, rounded pods, looking like fat zucchinis, hanging down below the palm fronds, much like a bunch of bananas. Most were green, but a few of the lowest among each bunch ranged from mottled green and orange to bright orange.

"Are those edible?" Jen asked eagerly. "Right now I'd eat about anything that won't poison me!"

"They're papayas," Chad answered, reaching up for one of the bright orange pods. "It's a fruit. You've seen them at the resort buffet. The brighter orange they are, the riper. The bunches grow down from the top of the tree, so the ripest are always on the bottom."

Chad handed me the papaya and reached for another. I had to use both hands to hold the fruit pod, which must have been a foot long. The skin was soft and yielding under my fingers.

"Levi, you got your knife?" Chad had already pulled off his backpack and was now taking out the knife he'd bought at the mission. Opening the blade, he cut the fruit he held in half lengthwise and gave half to Jen. Levi had taken my papaya and was doing the same. As he handed me half, I noticed the fruit was as bright orange as the skin. A hollow in the center was filled with black seeds.

"You don't eat the seeds, do you?" I asked.

"Well, they won't kill you," Chad replied. He had already scooped the seeds onto the ground and broken a big chunk of his half of papaya, gobbling the flesh from the skin as though eating a watermelon.

"Sorry, not trying to be rude," he mumbled around a mouthful. "I need to get this into my system—glucose plus liquid."

I hesitantly popped a seed—coated with a slimy membrane— into my mouth. I chewed, wrinkling my nose. "It tastes peppery. It may not be poisonous, but I don't think I'm going to eat the seeds."

Following Chad's example, I scooped out the rest of the seeds, wiping the slime they left on my fingers against a tuft of grass. Then I broke off a chunk, nibbling the fruit watermelon-style, though more neatly than Chad. I moaned with pleasure as the sweet juice trickled down my dry throat. If not quite as thirst-quenching as cold, bottled water, at least the fruit would tide me over.

Sinking to the ground, we all devoured the first two papayas, then Chad and Levi cut up two more. We finished them both. Chad was already looking much better, I noted with relief. Now if we could just find water.

"Let's check the building and see if we can find anything useful," I suggested. "Maybe even a well."

"Yes, we'd better get moving." Chad pushed himself to his feet. "And we should take a few of these papayas along. Who knows when we'll come across another meal!"

The papayas were big, and we could only fit one in each backpack without squashing the fruit. Jen had the bright idea of wrapping them first in palm fronds. We all had new bounce in our step, and even Jen was smiling as we headed toward the dilapidated building, not much larger than a shed with a thatched roof. I'd seen enough of Haiti now to know it had probably once housed a farm family.

The thatch was mostly gone, and debris had blown in through holes in the roof and walls, then built up in corners. I caught a glint of metal in one corner just before Jen pounced. She picked up a cylindrical object, then dropped it. "Yuck!"

I picked the object from the floor. Filthy and a bit rusted, it was also unmistakably a tin can, once used to hold a quart of peaches or tomatoes.

"I thought it might be a bucket," Jen said, grimacing with distaste, while wiping the rust and dirt on her fingers against her jeans. "No such luck."

"Actually, this is great luck," Chad said, lifting the can out of my hands and studying the sides and bottom. "If we do find a well or stream, we can wash it out and boil water. I don't see any holes."

Levi was already digging into the debris heap. He pulled out two more cans. One was rusted completely through on the bottom while the other was no bigger than ten ounces. I learned much about the poverty here—people keeping cans instead of throwing them away. Anything more valuable than a can didn't get abandoned in this economy.

"Well, at least we have a water container." I stood up, brushing debris from my jeans as though anything could improve their currently filthy condition. "Now we need water."

"Let's go look," Chad agreed. "Like you said, maybe there is a well since this was clearly a farm once. Or even an irrigation ditch. If not, we'll keep heading for the river."

Ducking his head through the low door of the shack, he stepped outside. The rest of us followed. We hadn't taken two steps away from the building when the whole earth seemed to let out a long, low burp.

This time I acted instinctively, racing away from the building until the shaking tripped me head-on. The shaking went on and on. I curled into a fetal position and covered my head with my arms, hoping the ground didn't open up and swallow me whole.

The shaking ceased as suddenly as it started. I pushed myself unsteadily to my feet and looked wildly around. "Levi! Chad! Jen!"

I let out my breath in relief as I spotted Levi and Jen picking themselves off the ground. Then I saw what two minutes before had been a ramshackle, but standing, shack, now a crumpled heap of boards and thatch. With a scream, I ran toward it, picking up boards and throwing them to the side. "Chad! Chad, where are you?"

Levi and Jen joined me in moving the rubble. We soon uncovered Chad, knocked face-first to the ground, blood trickling from a gash on his head. I dropped to my knees and shook him. "Chad!"

Chad stirred but didn't open his eyes. I shook him again.

"Chad!"

Levi knelt next to me. "He'll be okay. He's merely knocked out."

"What about his head? We don't have a first-aid kit. We don't even have anything clean to apply pressure with."

Levi pulled out his knife and reached for the blanket rope Chad had tied around his waist. I'd forgotten all about it. As he'd done for me, he cut off a length of the material.

I grabbed the material and pressed it to Chad's wound. "Guess this will have to do." Then I remembered to give Levi a smile. "Thanks, Levi. You saved the day again."

He smiled faintly back, then stopped smiling as the earth gave a slight shudder. Jen jumped to her feet, screaming up into the sky. "Enough already! Enough with the aftershocks!"

"Remember what Levi said. There was one ten days later in 2010," I said.

The longer Chad lay still and pale on the ground, the higher my anxiety climbed. "I wish he'd wake up."

"Even once he regains consciousness, he shouldn't walk anymore today," Levi said.

I turned to my twin. "Then we need to let him rest while you and I go on and try to find water. Jen can stay with Chad."

Levi nodded. "It's a good place. They can always pick more papayas."

"No!" Jen said. "I don't want to stay here. What if something happens?"

"If the kidnapper and his annoying nephew Stevens show up, grab one of those planks and whack them," I suggested.

"Funny." Jen's expression said it was anything but funny.

"Wait! Where's the can?" I looked wildly around. "Who had it when we came out?"

"I did. It's over here where I dropped it." Levi picked up the tin can, which had rolled a few feet away on the grass, and tucked it into his backpack, pulling out the papaya to make room.

Levi and I first searched around the collapsed shack for any sign of a well or pump. We found none nor an irrigation ditch or stream. By the time we'd given up and gone back to the others, Chad still wasn't conscious, though he seemed to be breathing easier and his head wound had stopped bleeding.

Levi shouldered his backpack, and I reached for mine. We really did need to go for water, but I dreaded splitting up. What if something did happen and we couldn't find each other again?

Jen voiced the same. "What if something happens? What if we lose each other?"

I swallowed hard. "Levi has his compass. We'll keep going northwest since that is where Chad said the river was. Once we find water, we'll head back southeast. We'll be back soon."

Jen didn't look convinced, and I couldn't blame her. As Levi and I set off, I was filled with a deep ache and a longing for Dr. and Mrs. M and the safety they represented. Were they even now out searching for us? Or had they been injured in the earthquake? Was the clinic still standing, or had it been destroyed?

Chapter Sixteen

As Levi and I hiked along, I tried to convince myself this would work out, and later we'd look back and remember how we'd all worked together to survive. But I was having a hard time convincing myself now. Little did I know what still lay ahead.

I strained to hear anything sounding like a river or even the trickle of a stream. But it was quiet. Too quiet. Only the sound of my breathing and an occasional comment from Levi broke the stillness, a sharp contrast from the noise of things falling during the earthquake.

After walking on fairly flat ground for a while, we headed down the side of the mountain again. I stopped short when I caught sight of a huge crack in the earth in front of us. I could guess this too was from the earthquake as it looked like the one where we hid from the kidnappers. This one was far deeper—deep enough the crevice floor was lost in the dark shadows.

Beside me, Levi was studying the depths calmly. "At least the crevice is narrow enough to jump. No more than three or four feet."

"Jump?" I felt lightheaded thinking about a jump. "What if we slip and fall? We can't even see how far down it is—maybe all the way to China!"

"Not possible. China isn't opposite Haiti on the globe." Levi was always logical. "Besides, we don't have a choice if we're going to get water for Chad. Listen!"

Following the direction of Levi's turned head, I strained to hear anything. A distant rushing sound somewhere beyond the crevice could be wind in the trees, but it could also be water.

Swallowing down my fear the best I could, I lectured myself sternly as I took a step forward. Don't be a wimp! Levi's right. I can make it.

But I stopped again on the edge of the crevice, dizziness making my head spin. I swayed and would have pitched forward if Levi hadn't reached out and pulled me back from the rim. My fingers felt icy cold against his warm hands. "Hey, it's okay," he said gently. "I'll go, and you can wait here for me. It can't be far if we can hear the water."

I looked at him in surprise, unused to my twin comforting me instead of the other way around. "No way! We go, we go together! We had to leave Chad and Jen behind, which was bad enough."

Again, I stepped forward. I had to do this, if not for me, then for Chad and for Levi. But I couldn't force myself across the gap. Thrusting my hands into my jean pockets, I looked over at Levi and burst out, "Why does all this have to happen now when we finally got a family? It doesn't seem fair."

Levi let out a sigh and dropped into a sitting position on the ground. "Let's rest a few minutes."

After a moment, I dropped down beside him. I felt something knobby and hard between me and the ground and reached into a pocket. I pulled out the nutmeg shell Dr. M had given me on the beach. I looked at it, rubbing my thumb back and forth against its ridges, then looked over at Levi.

"You know, when Dr. M gave me this, I told him my life has had lots of bumps and ridges too, but they sure don't make a cool pattern like this. He told me God can weave the pieces of my life into something as beautiful as this shell."

Levi held out his left hand, and I dropped the shell into his palm. He rubbed a forefinger over the ridges as he asked thoughtfully, "So do you think he could be right?"

I shrugged. "It sounds good, but if true, couldn't God have kept us from years of abusive homes? The ridicule? Being hit? Bullied?" A sigh escaped my lips. "I sure wish I could believe God could weave something beautiful from my life ... that he'd even want to. Dr. M says there's something missing in my life, and he hopes I find out what it is on this trip. But there's too much missing, a normal childhood being at the top of the list."

Levi had a faraway look on his face. Was he reliving the years of abuse? Then he sighed too. "We've got to remember the people who did the stuff to us—they're the ones with the real problems. We've got to get over what they did and get on with our lives."

I raised my eyebrows in surprise at my twin. Once again, he was comforting me instead of the other way around. "You're right. I'm being silly. But every time I'm faced with heights, I think about—you know, them!"

"The boys?"

I bit at my lip as I nodded. "What if that family had finished our adoption? What if we were stuck there forever?" A shudder passed through me.

"Don't think of them." Getting to his feet, Levi offered me his hand. "Let heights remind you we are survivors. Besides, we have a family now."

"If we ever see them again!" I said gloomily. I let him pull me to my feet.

"We will. Remember what Chad said this morning—stuff about confident hope. It made sense to me. I think I really believe him."

Levi handed me back the nutmeg shell. As I stuffed it into a pocket, he retreated a few feet from the crack in the ground. Breaking into a run, he jumped lightly over the crevice. He turned to face me. "Piece of cake! Come on! You can do it."

There was no more postponement. My breathing was

ragged as I fastened my backpack tighter around me, clinching the waist strap, then sidled back a few steps. I forced myself to look straight across at Levi instead of down into the crevice. Sucking in air to the count of ten, I slowly released the air, then charged forward.

I came down hard onto slippery ground. Without warning, my feet slid from under me, causing me to land on my bottom. But at least I was safely across the crevice. Scrambling to my feet, I smiled shakily at Levi, trying to force the tremble from my voice. "Whew. I sure don't want to do that again!"

"Me either," Levi agreed as he set off immediately toward the rushing sound. "But we have to go back the same way."

My shoulders slumped. Of course, we did! As Levi set the pace toward the rushing sound we'd heard earlier, I forced myself to think about my surroundings, not the crevice we had to cross back over. We were climbing again through thick brambles and trees. Soon the ground became moist under my feet. The encouragement of knowing we must be getting close gave me renewed energy for the steep scramble.

I called ahead to Levi. "Could this be the river already?"

Levi paused to glance back. "I don't know. I wouldn't think so from what Chad said, but I'll be happy to find any water."

As we climbed higher, the rushing sound grew louder. My heart lightened when I spotted water trickling down through the trees, and I began pushing ahead faster. A few minutes later, we emerged into the open to find ourselves standing at the foot of a small waterfall cascading over boulders into a small pool before forming a creek that spilled down the hillside.

Tugging off my backpack, I dropped to my knees beside the pool and scooped water into my mouth, then splashed it over my face and arms. Beside me, Levi was doing the same. I didn't stop until my thirst was slaked and I felt cool and clean again.

"That was wonderful!" I said at last, raising my head. "I

don't think I've ever been so thirsty."

"Sure is!" Levi's muffled voice responded. I looked over at him and burst into laughter. My twin had ducked his entire head into the pool, and was soaking wet, water streaming from his hair and face.

Only then did I remember all the warnings about drinking water here without boiling. I wiped my hand across my mouth. Levi read my thoughts as he so often did.

"I wouldn't worry about the water. It is a rain-fed stream high enough in the mountains there won't be any human contamination, so it should be okay."

I remembered our mission and jumped to my feet. "We'd better get water back to Chad. Do you have the can?"

Levi dug the tin can from his backpack and plunged it under the waterfall. It wasn't much water to take back for two people, but it was all we had. At least now we knew where to get more.

Levi shouldered his backpack, then carefully picked up the dripping can. I shouldered my own backpack, then stopped. "You mind if I get a picture before we leave? The waterfall and creek look so peaceful."

Levi shrugged. I pulled out my iPad and quickly snapped a picture. I didn't have time to format it for a poem, but I typed out some quick thoughts.

June 8
Water gently flowing
No cares in the world
Winding its way through the wild terrain
Peace among untamed land
Be still my heart
Be still my soul
Look to the creek
And follow its ways.

I wasn't sure if the words really conveyed my thoughts, but I could fix them later. I put my iPad away, and we turned to start back down the mountain, more slowly now so we wouldn't lose our footing and spill the water.

"You know the way back, right?"

Levi nodded and held up his compass. "Just reverse our course."

The sun was sinking low by the time we reached the crevice. Water sloshed from the can as Levi jumped across, but far less than I would have thought. Following him didn't seem so difficult this time, perhaps because knowing we had the water Chad so badly needed took my mind off the unmeasured depth below me.

By the time we'd crossed the flatter terrain on the far side of the crevice, the setting sun had turned to an orange glow, a patch of tall, palm-like trees ahead now casting eerie black silhouettes. I stopped in my tracks. "Those trees are creepy. Did we pass them before?"

"Maybe we went more west before and missed them." Levi's mouth formed an O as he looked at the misshapen trees.

"What?"

"Those are banana trees making such strange shapes. Bunches of bananas."

We walked to the trees. They actually looked like the palms that lined avenues in Florida, though not as tall, and the bananas curved upwards in tiers to form bunches as tall as me and as big around as Chad. Like the papayas earlier, the lowest tiers of bananas were beginning to ripen while the higher ones were still green.

My mouth dropped open. "Wow, I've never seen such huge bunches of bananas. Would we be considered stealing if we take a few?"

"Maybe. This has to be someone's farm with all these

bananas and papayas. I wish we could leave them money. But hopefully they'll understand this is an emergency. Let me get out my knife, and I'll cut a few down."

Carefully setting down the quart can of water, Levi slid his backpack from his shoulder and pulled out the multipurpose utility knife he'd purchased at the mission. He walked around to choose the ripest bunch, then sawed at the bottom tier until he could snap away a single bunch holding a half-dozen bananas.

He handed the bunch to me. "Here, you carry these, and I'll get the water."

Water and bananas in hand, we continued our journey back. By now the sun had completely set, and the first stars had emerged by the time we reached the abandoned farmhouse. We still had light enough to see across the yard with its earthquake debris—but no sign of humans. Where were Chad and Jen?

"Where did they go?" I demanded even though I knew Levi wouldn't have the answer.

He shrugged.

Concern overwhelmed me, and I screamed out their names. "Chad? Jen?"

A rustling to the right made me turn and look. Jen was running toward us. "Jeesh, Lexi, if the kidnappers are anywhere within ten miles, they heard you!"

Relief overrode my irritation at Jen. "Where were you?"

"We moved over by the trees. It's more sheltered. Chad has set up a big rock and piled wood around it for boiling water when you got back, even though I keep trying to get him to rest."

"He's okay?" The knot in my stomach lessened.

"No, but he thinks he is. You know how stubborn he can be."

I headed toward the place she'd indicated. I immediately spotted the wood piled around a flat stone. Chad was stretched out on the ground next to the stone, his eyes closed. Setting down the bunch of bananas, I broke into a run.

"Chad! Chad!" Dropping to my knees, I shook him.

He opened his eyes. "Water?"

"Yes. But we have to start a fire and boil it. It was a mountain stream, so Levi says it's probably clean enough, but we'd better not take a risk with your diabetes. We have bananas. Do you want one? Or another papaya? The juice should help you."

"Too tired," Chad said. "Just one quick drink."

I held the can to his lips while he took a few sips, then he rolled over and went back to sleep.

Darkness had now settled, so I pulled out my iPad and turned on the light. Levi looked at the pile of wood Chad had had gathered. "Chad has it almost ready. We can use my fire starter kit to get the fire going."

He opened the waterproof case and removed the flint starter, which looked a lot like a thumb drive with the ends plugged in to each other. He pulled the ends apart, exposing the metal end and the flint end. Then he tore open one of the cellophane pouches and pulled out a white cube. He scraped at the cube, and some shavings fell off.

Levi tried to strike the metal piece against the flint, but nothing happened.

"You have to do it faster," Jen said.

Levi's hands stopped moving. I glared at Jen, silently threatening her if she said another word.

"Can I try?" Jen asked, giving me an exaggerated, almost sarcastic, smile.

Shrugging, Levi dropped the fire starter kit and stepped away. Jen picked up the two ends of the fire starter and struck them together. A spark flickered. Jen looked startled. "I did it!"

I grinned at her surprise. "Yes, but you have to light the shavings with the spark. Then add those little twigs."

Jen struck the metal against the flint again, this time

lighting the shavings, and we had the start of a fire. We quickly added the twigs, followed by bigger branches.

The fire was started, and for now things were looking up.

Chapter Seventeen

The fire grew, providing enough light to see each other. Levi walked up with the can of water. Leaning in gingerly, he set the can on the flat stone in the middle of the fire. Chad had thought of everything. If we placed the can on the wood, it would tip over as the wood burned down.

"So how are we going to lift the can off once the water starts boiling?" Jen asked.

Levi pulled out his multipurpose knife and unfolded one of the attachments. "Pliers."

Jen stared at him. "You know, you've said more today than I've heard you say the whole trip."

Levi shrugged.

Locking eyes with Jen, I gave a small shake of my head. Levi talks fine if he feels comfortable with the people he's around. But if Jen said something Levi took as criticism, he'd stop talking again. I didn't want Levi to withdraw, because if we were going to get out of this, we all had to work together.

On the other hand, Levi hadn't shut down over starting the fire and had even let Jen have her little triumph. So maybe he was getting used to her—and her jabs.

"I guess we all do what we have to," Jen went on. "No one at home would believe I started a fire in the wilderness."

I didn't know how to answer, so we sat in silence as the water came to a boil. I looked at Levi. "How long do we boil it?"

Levi answered in the monotone of an answering service. "According to the Washington State Department of Health and the United States Environmental Protection Agency, to purify the water, you should bring it to boil and keep it rolling for one minute. At altitudes above one mile, or 1609.3 meters, you should increase the rolling time to three minutes."

Jen's mouth dropped open. "You remember all that?"

She looked reluctantly impressed. Levi didn't answer her. He was counting under his breath, and I knew he was counting off the three minutes. When he stopped, he opened the pliers, leaned in to grip the edge of the tin can, then lifted it away from the fire to the ground. I added more wood to the fire from the pile Chad had made to chase some of the darkness away.

"How long will it take to cool?" Jen addressed the question to Levi instead of me, indicating how much her impression of him had changed. "I am dying of thirst!"

Again, Levi didn't answer. He started digging around in his backpack, then thrust a small box at me.

"What's is it?" I asked.

"The tea I bought for Mom and Dad, but Chad can have it."

I tried to read the box by the glow of the fire. "It's in Creole. I have no idea what it says."

Opening the box, I pulled out several tea bags and dropped them into the can. There was still no sound from Chad, which worried me. Was he okay?

Levi pulled three bananas from the bundle. He handed one to me and one to Jen. We sat around the fire in silence, munching. For once it wasn't an awkward silence, but a silence born out of exhaustion and accomplishment.

Finishing my banana, I tossed aside the peel and glanced into the can. "I'd say the tea is steeped enough. I wish we had a cup. I guess we can sit Chad up, and he can sip from the container."

"I have an idea," Jen said. She picked another banana, peeled back the top, and carefully worked the fruit out of the peel. Then she turned to Levi. "Mind if I borrow your knife?"

Wordlessly, Levi passed his knife to her. She sliced through the peel half-way down and held out the bottom half, still in one piece. "Voila! Instant cup!"

My mouth dropped open. "I would have never thought of it."

Jen smirked. "I'm not totally helpless. Besides, I didn't really think it up. When we were on a cruise last year, a guy was drinking an alcoholic beverage out of a fancy version of a banana peel cup."

Levi and I each grabbed a banana and tried to copy Jen, but ours did not work out as well. Still, they were better than nothing. I dipped my banana peel cup into the bucket and scooped out a bit of tea. I took a sip. I'd clearly put in far too many tea bags. "Oh, this is horrible! The banana taste helps a bit, though."

Jen and Levi tried some, and for once we all agreed on something. The tea was horrible. Still, we needed to get Chad hydrated, so I filled my peel cup with tea, careful not to burn my fingers. "You guys help him sit up. I'll hold the cup to his mouth."

Jen went over and shook Chad. Levi got behind Chad to support him. I held the tea to his lips. "Try to drink this. It's horrible, but it's made with water."

Chad took a sip. "Augh. Are you trying to poison me?"

Relief flooded me. If Chad was able to joke around, he must be feeling better. "It's the best we could do with Levi's souvenir tea and banana peels."

Levi handed one of the peeled bananas to Chad, who took a bite. I held the tea to his mouth again. Chad grimaced but drank a few more sips.

"I wonder what Dr. M would think of this," I said.

"He'd think you were pretty clever to use banana peels," Chad replied.

"It was Jen's idea."

Chad raised his eyebrows. "Really?"

"I copied something I saw on a cruise."

Chad turned to me. "Did you take pictures?"

I looked at him. "Of what?"

"Our fancy banana peel teacups, of course." Chad held his cup with his pinky up in an exaggerated gesture. "See, I could have tea with the queen."

Jen rolled her eyes, but I took the picture of Chad with my iPad anyway—and one of Jen's expression too.

We broke open a papaya to complete our supper. The juicy flesh washed away the bitter taste of too-strong tea. Chad was thirsty enough to finish most of the tea, too strong or not.

The fire was dying down by now, the night closing in around us. I didn't want to waste any more of the iPad battery, so we all agreed to turn in. I lay down and used my backpack as a pillow. At least the ground was flat, and the thick grass was soft.

Soon, Levi's and Jen's deep breathing and Chad's snores told me they were asleep, but I lay awake on my back, looking into the night sky. Emptiness filled me, and an ache grabbed hold of my heart. How could I feel so alone while I was with my twin, Chad, and Jen? Was this what Dr. M was talking about when he said something was missing from my life? Was that absence what made me ache with loneliness even when surrounded by three relatives?

Dots of light sparked overhead, and the vastness of the night sky overwhelmed me. Tears ran silently down my cheeks. I rolled on my side to look at Levi, a dark shape in the darkness beside me. I envied him. He was doing so well at handling the situation. I'd expected him to have a major meltdown and not be able to help at all. Instead, he'd been the one to find the water and get us safely back to the others. He had a fire-starter kit and knew how long to boil the water.

I was tempted to wake up Levi to tell him about the vast emptiness in me, but he might not have understood. He seemed to think all the bad years were behind us, the Michaels were our forever family and the solution to all our problems.

Instead, I pulled the shell from my pocket and closed my hand around it. Was Dr. M right about God making something beautiful out of the junk in my life? I looked up at the star-studded night sky. "Are you up there? Is there a plan for all this mess?"

Only silence answered me. I sighed, rolled over, and willed myself to sleep.

Chapter Eighteen

Hunger woke me, followed by thirst and the need for a private bush. I sat up and looked around. The others were still asleep, but birds were welcoming the morning with their melodies.

I found a private area, then returned to the group. By the time I got back, Chad was awake and on his feet. He moved more slowly than usual, the energetic gait missing from his step.

"Are you okay?" I asked.

He grimaced. "Better, but not good. In case I didn't say it last night, thanks for getting water for me."

"I'm glad we found some." I made a banana peel cup for Chad, handing him the banana and filling the peel with tea. Less than an inch remained by the time I finished pouring.

I peeled another for myself as he drained the cup, then ate the banana. By now Jen and Levi were awake. Pushing back tussled hair, Jen complained, "I'm thirsty again. But I'm not drinking any more tea!"

"We'll have to go for more water." Chad pulled a papaya from his backpack. He pulled out his knife and cut off the top third of the huge fruit. "If we're careful scooping out the seeds and flesh, this might make a decent water container."

After using his fingers to pull out the black seeds, Chad carved out reddish-orange chunks, being careful to leave the shell about a half inch thick. By the time we'd devoured the juicy flesh, we were no longer thirsty, and the papaya was a hollow container shaped much like a vase. I picked it up and peered inside, amazed at how inventive we could be when we had to.

A bird call drew Levi's attention to the tree branches overhead. "Did you know there are over eighty species of birds in this part of Haiti? Would you like to know what they are?"

Jen turned and stared at him. "Can you name all eighty?"

Levi nodded. "I think so, if you want to hear their names."

"No, that's okay." Jen's sarcastic tone set me on edge, but subtleties normally alluded Levi. He wasn't good at reading a person's face to gauge their feelings or getting clues from their tone of voice.

I looked at Levi to see how he was reacting to Jen, but he was watching a bird flit from one branch to another. Maybe I was more bothered by Jen than Levi was. Was I so accustomed to fighting his battles that I'd become over-protective?

Then I noticed Chad had closed his eyes and was leaning back against a tree. Unease filled me as I spoke up. "I think we should move to the stream we found yesterday until Chad is ready to go on, so we'll have water. We can pick more bananas on the way for food."

Chad immediately opened his eyes and sat up straight. "I'm okay. I can travel. The kidnappers are probably out looking for us right now, so we need to keep moving. Besides, Mom and Dad will be worried sick. We've been missing all night, and with the earthquake, they'll be imagining all kinds of terrible things have happened to us. We've got to get to the clinic. Not only so we'll be safe from the kidnappers, but so we can let Mom and Dad know we're okay."

"He's right," I agreed. "We don't even know if the kidnappers have contacted them yet or not. But we've got to get to them before they end up paying ransom because they think we're in trouble."

"We *are* in trouble!" Jen interjected.

I frowned at her. "You know what I mean! And we need to get the video with the kidnapper to them also. And to the police. Maybe someone will be able to identify and arrest him."

Levi spoke up. "The kidnapper knew Mom and Dad. Remember what he said about being glad we had good memories of them because he didn't?"

"Well, when we get back, Uncle David and Aunt Maggie can tell us why the guy's so mad at them," Jen said impatiently. "But Lexi's right. For now, let's just worry about getting to water and making sure Chad's thoroughly hydrated before we go any further. After all, we don't know what we'll be facing once we leave here, and we'd hate to have him collapse along the way."

My mouth dropped open, and Jen gave me a haughty look. "What? You didn't think I could care about anyone but myself?"

I felt heat rising up my neck and knew my skin was turning pink. Had she read my thoughts?

Chad eyed his cousin up and down with a grin. "You do come across a bit self-absorbed at times."

"Well, listen to you spouting off vocabulary like 'a bit self-absorbed'!" Jen mocked. "You been listening to morning talk shows or something?"

Chad's grin grew wider. "I thought it sounded better than, 'You can sure be a selfish brat at times!'"

"Thanks a lot!" Jen huffed. "Remember, I am the one who started the fire last night and invented the banana peel teacups."

"You're right! And we do appreciate your enormous contributions, don't we?" Chad looked around, and Levi and I both nodded. Anything to restore the peace and get on our way.

We quickly packed the remaining bananas and papayas in our backpacks. We each had one last swallow of tea, then headed the direction Levi and I had hiked the day before. When we reached the wide crack in the ground, the width and depth felt far less frightening than the day before. Maybe because this time the angle of the sun permitted a glimpse of the bottom, not nearly as far down as I'd pictured.

Following Jen at a quick run and jump over the crevice, I congratulated myself for not making a scene. Maybe I was finally getting over my fear of heights. Or depths. Levi made a quick check of his compass, and we embarked on the uphill climb through dense brush and trees. I knew we must be getting close to the waterfall when the ground grew damp again underfoot.

"Stop! Stop!" Jen's frantic shout froze us all in our tracks. Levi and Chad turned back. Behind her, I took in her up-and-down hopping motion, one knee and foot in the air. Had she been bit by a snake?

Then I saw what was in her hand. Still hopping, she waved her sandal in the air. "My strap broke! Now what am I supposed do? These sandals were expensive too!"

Levi unzipped his backpack and began digging through the contents.

"Don't tell me he has a spare sandal in there," Jen said, a hint of sarcasm edging her voice.

I glanced at Levi, but he seemed not to have heard her. He pulled out an almost empty roll of camouflage duct tape. I guess there are advantages to having an autistic twin who picks up odds and ends others would never notice.

Jen gingerly lowered her bare foot to the ground, balancing the sandal on the tips of her toes as she gaped at Levi. "Duct tape! I'm supposed to duct tape my sandal? These cost over $100!"

I stared at her. "A hundred dollars? For sandals?"

"Yes, they're name-brand. I didn't expect to go hiking through the wilderness in them. They match my bag." She held up her flowered bag, then, seeing how filthy it was, she wrinkled her nose in disgust.

Chad looked from Jen to the duct tape and back. "Well, you have two choices. Duct tape the sandal to your foot or risk walking barefooted."

Jen wrinkled her nose. "Oh great! Like I really have a choice at all."

Chad took the tape from Levi. While Jen held the sandal in place, Chad secured it to her foot using Levi's roll of tape. When he finished, Chad cut off the excess. "Do you want me to do the other one so you don't lose it too?"

"May as well," Jen shrugged. "Great. Matching duct-taped sandals."

Chad taped the second sandal and handed the tape back to Levi. "Okay, let's get moving!"

When I saw how hard Chad was breathing as we climbed uphill, I was glad for the break, whatever the reason. He was bending over and holding his side by the time we broke into the open and saw the waterfall ahead.

We all rushed toward the pool, and Jen was right beside me as we both shucked off our backpacks and dropped to our knees to duck our faces and hands into the cool water. Precautions like boiling water didn't even enter my mind as I drank my fill. But when I lifted my dripping face, I heard Chad and Levi in serious discussion.

"You're right." Chad's gaze followed Levi's uphill to where a rushing thread of water spilled down a narrow gully and over the waterfall to continue down the hillside. "The water's coming from way up the mountain, so it has to be clean rainwater. I think it should be safe enough to drink."

Levi produced the quart can from the depths of his backpack, plunged it under the waterfall, and handed it to Chad. I dug into my own backpack, lifting out our hollowed-out papaya "canteen," now a bit bruised and dented in my backpack but still intact. I filled it under the waterfall, then set it carefully against a tree trunk so it wouldn't spill.

Chad was still breathing hard. Jen gave him a sharp glance before announcing, "I'm going to need to rest before I go on. This is a good a place for a break."

Plopping to the ground, she dug a banana from her backpack, peeled it, broke it in half, and held a half toward Chad. "Here, this is more than I can eat, so you might as well finish it off."

Sinking to the ground beside his cousin, Chad took the banana and ate it, then leaned against a rock and closed his eyes. I knew what Jen was up to and gave her a grateful look as Levi and I joined the other two on the ground. Self-absorbed she might be, but she really did care about Chad.

Chad's breathing gradually slowed, and after a while, he opened his eyes and sat up straight. Reaching for the tin can, he filled it and took a long drink. "Okay, I'm good, Let's move on."

"Are you sure?" I asked.

Before he could answer, a murmur of voices drifted toward us through the trees. We all stared at each other in shock before scrambling to our feet and grabbing our backpacks.

"We've got to find a place to hide," Chad hissed.

"What if it's someone who could help us?" Jen hissed back. "Maybe the ones farming those bananas and papayas?"

Chad shook his head. "And what if it isn't? We should get out of sight in case."

He started down the hillside at a fast pace, and the rest of us followed, dodging through brush and around trees. The sound of voices had stopped, and after a hard, fast scramble downhill brought us out into the open and onto more level ground, Chad slowed our pace.

"False alarm," he called over his shoulder. "Whoever it was, I think we lost them."

Just then, a shout rang out behind us. Another shouted back.

By now none of us could mistake those voices. We'd been seen, and this was not a rescue party!

Chapter Nineteen

"Run!" I screamed unnecessarily since all of us were already attempting to dash over the rubble and uneven terrain. I resisted the urge to look back, knowing it would only slow me. From the sound of their shouts retreating into the distance, we had a growing lead on the kidnappers, but only if we kept running. And how long could Chad keep up in his condition?

How long could I keep running? I was already breathing hard, a stitch in my side becoming more painful at every stride. Adrenaline kept me running until Levi suddenly stopped right in front of me. I skidded to a stop before bumping into him.

"What is it?" I asked. Then I let out a gasp as Levi stepped aside so I could see.

Ahead of us, the terrain broke away into a deep gorge. If Levi hadn't stopped, we'd likely have raced right over the edge. And unlike the crevice I'd been so terrified of earlier, this one was far too wide to jump—at least twenty feet across—while the tangle of green vegetation I could see at the bottom was a sheer drop a good fifty feet straight down.

I could feel the usual panic and dizziness sweeping over me as I stared into the awful depth. I could also hear the shouts of the kidnappers, closer than they'd been. We were trapped!

Then Levi grabbed my hand. "Come on!"

He was tugging me to the right along the gorge rim. From the corner of my eye, I saw Jen and Chad keeping pace beside us before I realized where Levi was pulling me and yanked to a stop again. A few more yards ahead, a dirt-like bridge, no more than a yard wide and covered in mossy vegetation, spanned the gorge. Stalactites overgrown with vines hung from the bottom.

"Are you kidding me?" I exclaimed. "The thing's made of dirt! We can't cross!"

Chad was now passing us, Jen on his heels. "Yes, we can!" he shot at me over his shoulder. "If it is dirt, it would have collapsed under its own weight. And we don't have a choice—unless you see any other way to cross!"

As Chad headed out onto the bridge, Levi grabbed my hand again. "Come on! We'll go together!"

Chad was already halfway across with Jen right behind him. I glanced back. The kidnappers were now in sight, running full-out toward us, no more than a hundred yards away. I could either cross the bridge now or be recaptured. Worse, I would be getting Levi recaptured too.

As though taking for granted I would follow, Levi stepped out onto the bridge. I kept my eyes on his back as I stepped out after him. Chad and Jen had now reached the other side.

If Jen can, so can I! I told myself fiercely. Levi took another step, and I did too. Then another. Behind us, renewed shouts told me the kidnappers had seen what we were doing and were gaining on our lead.

"Hurry!" I told Levi. He quickened his pace, and so did I.

We were almost to the far side when I felt a slight tremor shake the bridge. I screamed and fell to my knees. My gaze dropped to the terrifying drop below us.

"Go!" Jen screamed from the bank. "Get out of there now!"

Levi turned back. "Grab my hand!"

Even as he yanked me to my feet, I could feel the bridge disintegrating beneath my feet.

"Run! Run!" Jen shouted. "The bridge is going!"

As though we weren't aware! Levi practically dragged me the last few feet. No sooner had we cleared the bridge than the dirt, moss, stone, and whatever else spilled into the gorge below. As I realized how close we'd come to joining the rubble at the bottom of the gorge, a shudder passed through me, and I began to tremble.

Angry shouts brought me out of my fear. The kidnappers had reached the other side and were screaming with fury at the sight of the collapsed bridge. And with a sheer rock face below them, they now had no way to cross. At least some good had come from our close call.

As though with one mind, we all hurried away from the gorge until we could no longer see the kidnappers. A well-trodden path led through the brush and trees, probably trampled down by animals or even people crossing the bridge.

We heard no sound from our pursuers. They must be searching for a way across the gorge. The relief allowed us to slow down. Once I'd recovered my breath from the desperate race, I looked over at Chad. "That bridge could just as easily have fallen with you and Jen. We could have all died back there. And you wonder why I don't like heights!"

Chad grinned at me. "But we didn't fall. Doesn't that tell you something?"

"Tell me something?"

"How do you know that was God?" Jen demanded. "What if Mother Nature was throwing a fit, and good luck was the only reason we weren't killed?"

Chad laughed. "It's a faith thing. You'll see."

"Hmmph!" Jen didn't look convinced. As we continued walking, she glanced sideways at me. "So what's your story? What happened to you?"

I gave her a blank stare as though I had no idea what she was talking about. "What happened when?"

"The heights thing!" Jen said impatiently. "We'd have to be blind not to notice you've got a problem with heights. What started your fear?"

I shrugged. "Something doesn't always have to happen for a person to have fears," I said.

Ahead on the path, Chad turned to raise his eyebrows at me. "Uh-huh? Come on, Sis. We're going to find out sooner or later."

I bit my lip. "Okay, fine! It happened at the other family who were going to adopt us——a man, his wife, and two older teen boys."

I stopped and swallowed, unable to go on. To my surprise, Levi spoke up. "They were creeps! Anytime their parents weren't around, they hit us, made fun of us, took what little stuff we had, figured out new ways to torment us."

"And the heights?" Jen prompted.

He looked over at me. I answered reluctantly, "The mom wasn't so bad. She gave Levi and me a kitten. Those—" I bit back the name I wanted to call them. "—creeps put the kitten on the garage roof."

Jen looked appalled. "Why would they do that? Who would hurt a kitten? Makes no sense."

"Meanness doesn't have to make sense," Chad spoke up. "Bullies don't follow the same rules as everyone else."

I nodded. "I think they were mean only to freak out Levi and me. And it worked. I found a ladder, climbed to the roof, and got the kitten. But when I stepped back onto the ladder, they pulled it away from the garage. So, only they were holding the ladder with me on it. Then they started swinging the ladder back and forth. Levi tried to make them stop."

I glanced over at my twin. The pain in his eyes told me he still felt grief over his failure, and I added hastily, "It wasn't Levi's fault. They were big mean guys. I tried to hold the kitten with one hand and the ladder with the other, but I couldn't. They shook the ladder so hard I fell and broke my arm."

"And the kitten?" Jen demanded.

I stared down at the path, walking several more paces before I finally answered. "Well, let's just say Levi didn't speak a word for over six months. Thankfully, he and I don't always need words to communicate."

Under her breath, Jen muttered a word I knew she didn't use around Dr. M. I threw her a half-smile. "You don't have to try and think of the right thing to say. There are no words to describe those creeps without getting grounded for a month. The good news is the hospital reported my injury to social services, and we were moved to a different house the same day. At least we were saved from being adopted by that family."

Jen looked even more outraged. "Did the parents know what their sons were doing?"

I shrugged. "They probably saw what they wanted to see—like everyone else."

Chad shook his head. "Crazy! Do you think you'll ever be okay with heights again?"

I shrugged again. "Who knows? I didn't mind heights before. But today sure hasn't helped!"

Levi had tuned the conversation out, as he did when sad memories were involved. He was checking his compass. "Over there should be the river we crossed in the van."

We were taking our time now the kidnappers were safely behind us, letting Chad recover his strength. Okay, maybe not just Chad. After another quarter hour, we heard the unmistakable sound of rushing water.

"Another waterfall!" I exclaimed happily. I couldn't be the only one who was thirsty again, and we'd lost both the tin can and our papaya "canteen" in our mad dash from the last waterfall.

"Or maybe it's the river," Jen offered, "meaning we're almost there, right?"

Chad shook his head. "The river wouldn't be so noisy. Not unless there's major rapids involved—which we sure didn't see when we crossed before. But we're heading in the right direction. Either way, it can't be too much further.

With renewed spirits, we followed Levi. The rushing sound grew louder as we went. At least there was a promise of water. I determined I'd stay brave no matter what we faced. After all, we'd come this far against all odds of kidnappers, earthquakes, and collapsing bridges. Was Chad right in believing this was some sort of sign and God was protecting us?

The terrain suddenly opened up, and for the first time we could see what was making the rushing sound. It was the river after all, but not the calm, placid, meandering stream we had crossed the day before.

"Are you sure this is the same river?" I asked incredulously, staring at the surging, angry torrent.

A glance at the others let me know they were as shocked at the river's appearance as I was. A tree rushed by, buffeted on the raging water. It turned sideways, jamming between the banks and stopping abruptly several yards down the river from us.

"Wow! Crazy!" Chad gestured at the river. "The earthquake could have shifted the river's course. Add crashing rocks and trees, and this is what you get, I guess."

But the river wasn't the only terrifying sight now we were in the open. Up the riverbank from us, the kidnapper and Stevens were picking their way across a field of fresh debris and rocks that looked as though they were deposited there by the earthquake.

"Oh no! Look!"

Whether they'd already spotted us, or my stupid outburst had alerted them, the kidnapper and his nephew were now calling out and pointing our direction. I saw a gun in the kidnapper's hand as a shot rang out above the noise of the rushing river.

The shot must have been intended as a warning as it came nowhere near us. But if the kidnapper thought the shot would make us freeze, he was wrong. Chad began running toward the river, and we all followed. Overflowing water made the path slippery and treacherous.

What are we doing? I asked myself as I scrambled and slipped. This time there wasn't even a rock bridge!

"Look!" Chad yelled over his shoulder. "A downed tree right where we need to cross the river. Head for the tree. We can push it free once we're across and leave them stranded on this side."

We had actually gained on the kidnappers by the time we reached the jammed tree because they were having to pick their way across the landslide, and they hadn't tried firing their gun again. But my heart sank as we reached the mass of fallen branches. I'd freaked out on what now seemed a nice, wide, solid bridge of earth. This was too much!

God, if you're really watching us, how can you ask me to do this again? I screamed upward even as I scrambled after Chad and Jen, Levi behind me. Was this some kind of cosmic joke? Let's get the girl who's scared of heights? I followed as he sped toward the tree, only minutes earlier jammed between the banks. He wanted to cross on that?

Just as before, the alternative was letting the kidnappers catch up to us, so I stepped out cautiously after the other two, Levi crowding my heels. As I glanced back toward the bank, I saw two things that amped up my already high anxiety level.

First were the angry faces of the kidnappers as they reached the end of the landslide and broke into a run. The other was a second tree careening down the river straight toward us.

"Watch out!" I screamed.

Before anyone could react, the second tree crashed into the

one we were on, knocking it free of the bank. I grabbed at a branch but was pitched into the water. A glancing blow from one of the trees or a branch knocked me under. I tumbled over and over in the raging current as I fought to reach the surface.

I finally broke the surface, coughing and gagging and spewing out rancid water as I fought to right myself. But the current was relentless, and I was carried headfirst downriver with no way to slow myself.

Chapter Twenty

Going headfirst down a rushing river isn't good. I remembered when Dr. and Mrs. M took us whitewater rafting a few months ago. We were instructed that if we fell out of the raft we should lie on our backs and put our feet in front of us. That way we'd hit submerged rocks with our feet, not our heads.

This knowledge was no help at the moment. I was nothing more than a rag doll being pitched about. Had I truly escaped the kidnappers only to die in the river anyway? Which was worse?

Where was Levi? And Chad and Jen? I could see nothing but roiling, brown water.

I shut everything from my mind except what I needed to do. My survival required keeping my head above water. At least I wasn't crashing against any boulders. After what seemed an eternity of tumbling and tossing like a washing machine, the river current slowed enough for me to get into the feet-first position. I had to focus all my effort on staying that way.

I rounded a curve. Ahead of me, I could see where part of the river widened into a calm, flat surface. If I could only maneuver my way into the still water! I kicked, trying to get to the edge of the water, fearing I'd never reach it.

Then as though the river had decided to spew me out, I found myself floating gently toward the bank. I put my feet down and discovered mud under my sneakers. Sloshing to the edge, I pulled myself out.

A new panic gripped me. Where were the others? Was I

ahead of them, or had they been pulled past this spot, unable to get out? Or were they even still—no, I wouldn't let my thoughts go there! They had to be okay. Especially my twin.

I knew the clinic was somewhere downriver, but I had no idea how far from here, what side of the river it was on, or even if I'd already swept past it. I tried to formulate a plan in my mind. If the others didn't show up in the next half hour, I'd have to head out and hope I'd run into someone who might help me. But then again, I didn't speak any Creole, and I wasn't good at pantomime.

At least I'd lost the kidnappers. But then I'd thought that before. Maybe I should find a good hiding place until I was sure the kidnappers had stopped searching.

My mind was still frantically kicking around ideas when I saw Chad rounding the curve. I waved my arms, screaming his name. Chad fought his way to the eddy but remained in the river. "Have you seen Jen and Levi? They were behind me last I saw."

Moments before I'd been relieved to get out of the river, but now concern for Levi overwhelmed me. And Jen, of course, but my twin was the one I cared most about. We'd faced so much together. I couldn't lose him now!

"Levi!" I screamed out, as if it would make any difference. Thankfully, Chad was clearheaded enough to actually do something useful. Somehow, he had managed to keep hold of the blanket rope from our escape, and now he stood waist-deep in the river with the rope wound up in one hand and ready to throw.

Jen and Levi came around the curve yards apart. Chad tossed the rope sideways so it would come within Levi's reach. Levi grabbed it and held tight. By the time Chad pulled him to safety, Jen had fought her way to the eddy on her own.

We all stood on the riverbank, dripping and disheveled, but

alive.

"I guess all those years of swim lessons were good for something," Jen joked, but the quiver in her voice gave away her real emotions.

"Everyone okay?" Chad asked.

We nodded.

"My bag is long gone," Jen said. "Too bad I didn't have a backpack like you guys. Then I would have had shoulder straps and a waist strap."

"You can replace your bag when you get home," Chad said. "At least we are all still alive. Now let's keep moving."

"What?" Jen sputtered. "We haven't been through enough for the day?"

"We don't know where the kidnappers are," Chad said.

"But they're on foot," Jen said. "We were swept way downstream, so they should be way behind us. And they can't know where we came ashore."

"But they also must have figured out by now we're headed to the clinic, the logical place for us to go, especially since the city is the opposite direction. If they decided there's no point in trying to keep following us, they may head straight there. Which means we've got to beat them to the clinic."

"So where is the clinic from here?" I asked.

"Depending on how far off course we are now," Chad answered, "it should be straight downriver from here. Where we landed here should be on the clinic side of the river if I've calculated right."

Chad turned and headed along the riverbank, the rest of us following. I jogged to catch him. "Do you really think we can get there without the kidnappers catching up to us?"

Chad glanced over at me. "Confident hope. Remember?"

"Confident hope?" Jen said from behind us. "What are you talking about?"

Chad quickly explained the verse to her the way he had to me.

Her mouth dropped open. "You believe even with all that's happened?"

Chad nodded. "We crossed the dirt bridge before it fell. We found water and fruit. And God definitely jammed a tree in the river right where we needed it. We all made it safely to shore, and now we're headed straight to the clinic. Even if everything hadn't gone right, I'd still believe God was in control. But I'm definitely glad he's worked things in our favor so far."

Chad had confidence in God, but like the rest of us, he had no clue what was still ahead.

Chapter Twenty-One

Chad kept us moving at a quick pace. Soon we reached a path, and then the path became a wider trail, which opened onto a dirt road. We could hear commotion in the distance.

"We must be nearing a village," Chad said. "Stay close together."

Weary, but with renewed spirits, I followed on Chad's heels, with Jen and Levi close on either side. We entered a typical Haitian village—small houses of mud, brick, and cinderblock; people in the streets; donkeys, goats, and pigs wandering around.

We immediately realized the earthquake had reached here too. Glass windows were broken, walls had huge cracks or were completely toppled. One entire building had collapsed, spilling debris far into the street. Men, women, and even children were sorting through the rubble. Other people sat along the roadside as though in despair, some talking, others were silent.

I pulled my phone from the waterproof pouch, but there was still no service. "So much for calling Dr M."

"Let's see if we can find a ride to the clinic," Chad suggested.

His words brought a new worry to my mind. I'd been thinking in terms of staying ahead of the kidnappers on foot. But if we could find a ride straight to the clinic, they could do so even more easily. How many miles back to the house where we'd been held? And they had both the black car and the resort van. It seemed we'd been running forever, but the actual distance wasn't really far. What if they'd already made it back to a vehicle and could drive straight to the clinic to cut us off?

No, I was worrying for nothing. It would take hours for the kidnappers to get back to their vehicles. By then, we would surely be at the clinic, and everything would be okay again. Dr. M would call the police, the kidnappers would be arrested, and we'd be safe.

A large, black pig dashed across our path, and I jumped, my heart racing. I hated how jittery I was. How long would it take me to get over the kidnapping and earthquake? Would any of us ever be the same?

Only a few vehicles were maneuvering through the broken glass, concrete, and other debris, making an obstacle course of the dirt road through town. My heart raced every time I saw a black vehicle.

Chad was trying to talk to the people sorting through debris. I couldn't understand, but I recognized the name of the town near the clinic. Each time, they would shake their heads and continue on with their work. Finally, one man turned to the other men, who were working to remove a collapsed brick wall from the street and repeated the name. A conversation followed with a lot of gesturing and rapid Creole.

Chad turned back to Jen, Levi, and me. "I don't understand half of it, but I think they are trying to find us a way to the town."

A man tapped Chad and gestured to another man with a snake tattoo on his arm. Chad walked over to the man, and they conversed, using more gestures than words. Chad turned to us. "This man will take us to the town. I told him we had no money, but he said he will do it for my backpack and the new knife I bought at the mission. The backpack alone is worth more than taxi fare by a long shot."

Even though Levi and I had special backpacks with waterproof pouches, given to us by Dr. M, Chad's was a state-of-the-art travel daypack guaranteed to be waterproof and rip-proof, with all kinds of ingenious pockets and compartments inside and out. He had saved for months to get it for this trip, so I knew how hard it had to be to trade away.

Chad was already pulling extraneous items from his backpack—a wadded handkerchief, his insulin supplies, his empty wallet and cellphone, a few trail-mix bar wrappers. All the food and water he'd carried was, of course, already gone. I unzipped my bag for him to stuff the items inside.

The tattooed man glanced inside the backpack, grunted satisfaction, then gestured for us to follow him to a rusty pickup truck parked along the edge of the street. Interpreting his hand motions as instructions to climb in, I stepped on the rear bumper and pulled myself into the pickup bed. Something flew at me, and I shrieked before realizing several chickens were fluttering around the pickup bed.

The man laughed and said something rapidly in Creole. He then shooed the chickens into a wire cage and shut the door. They clucked in protest as I settled against the side of the pickup bed. Levi sat beside me—Chad and Jen sat across from us.

With a lurch, the truck pulled into the road, maneuvering like an obstacle course around pigs, debris, and milling people. I looked over at Chad. "Do you think we'll have to leave Haiti, or will Dr. and Mrs. M stay to help with the crisis?"

Chad shrugged. "They'll want to stay and help, but they'll be worried about us."

I grimaced. "Could it be any worse than what we've already gone through?"

We bumped along dirt roads and through villages also bearing signs of the earthquake damage, though not as extensive as the first. It was a hopeful sign the quake might not have reached as far as the clinic.

The pickup truck slowed as we entered another village,

undamaged but depressingly poor. The houses were no more than shacks cobbled together from planks and mud brick with lengths of corrugated tin for roofs. Leaning out the window, the driver shouted something in Creole. Chad shouted back, and the truck pulled over to the side of the road.

Climbing down from the cab, the tattooed man came around back and gestured at the backpack Chad still held.

"What's going on?" I asked. "Are we already to the clinic?"

Chad handed over the backpack and climbed out. "Not quite. But this is the village where he agreed to take us. The clinic is up there—see?"

Following his gesture, I could see a dirt driveway leading through trees to a glimpse of a high, light-blue wall. The tattooed driver was already climbing back into his cab, backpack in hand. We chorused our thanks as he backed the pickup truck to turn around.

We headed for the driveway as the truck sped away, leaving a cloud of dust behind. With each step forward, I felt a bit more of the hope Chad had talked about. Unbelievably, we had actually made it—at least in a few more steps.

Once we reached the dirt driveway, I could see a double gate of solid metal panels set in the compound wall. A smaller rectangle in the right-hand panel denoted the typical pedestrian door I'd seen in other gates since we'd arrived in Haiti. We all exchanged relieved grins as we started down the driveway.

Just then, the rumble of the departing pickup truck was drowned by the roar of a racing engine. As I swung around, a small, black compact emerged from the cloud of dust raised by the pickup. If I couldn't see the driver clearly, there was no mistaking the man leaning out the window behind the driver's seat.

Or the gun he brandished.

Chapter Twenty-Two

"Run!" Chad shouted.

All four of us broke into a dash toward the gate as Chad shouted in Creole. I didn't need to speak the language to know he was yelling at the compound watchman to open the gate.

Looking over my shoulder as I ran, I saw the black compact overshoot the driveway, then come back into sight in reverse, dirt and rocks flying as the car made a sharp turn into the driveway.

By now the pedestrian gate was swinging open. An elderly, dark-skinned man with a wrinkled face, white hair, and a rifle slung across his shoulders peered out before standing aside to let us in. Chad shoved Jen and me in ahead of him, with Levi on his heels. He then swung around to slam the pedestrian gate shut and slap the metal deadbolt into the slot.

Outside the gate, car doors slammed, followed by the sound of furious men shouting, shouting in Creole. I tensed, expecting pounding on the gate or even shots. Instead, there was more slamming of car doors, then revving of an engine. Spotting a narrow slit in the pedestrian door—clearly a peephole—I stepped close to peer out, just in time to see the black compact reverse down the drive, then speed out of sight.

Meanwhile, Chad was chattering away in Creole with the guard, whose perplexed look gradually turned to horror, then anger. The guard spoke in turn, hands waving in agitation. When he stopped speaking, Chad turned around to the rest of us.

"This is Samuel, the compound watchman. I explained what happened to us and the men in the car out there were our kidnappers. He hadn't heard anything about our disappearance, but he said a man came late afternoon the day before yesterday. He had an urgent message for Dad and Mom, and they went off with him. They haven't been back to the clinic since."

Jen spoke up. "That must have been one of the kidnappers, or someone they sent to demand the ransom. But why would Uncle David and Aunt Maggie go with him? They should have grabbed him and called the police!"

"Mom and Dad would do about anything if the kidnappers threatened to hurt us," Chad responded soberly. "Let's go into the clinic and see if someone there knows anything more. And we should call the resort to let them know we're okay. Maybe Mom and Dad are back there by now."

Chad led the way across a dusty, packed-earth courtyard to a long, cinderblock building with a verandah along the front. Since it was mid-morning by now, I was rather surprised to see no sign of lined-up patients or clinic staff. But when we entered a small room, I saw a tall, big-boned Haitian woman in white scrubs and cap sorting through a supply cabinet. After a short conversation in Creole, Chad translated for the rest of us.

"Angelina is the clinic administrator. The clinic is closed today because of the earthquake. The local doctor and other personnel are out helping with relief efforts. Angelina stayed behind to care for a handful of cases too ill to be outpatients. She says they haven't heard from Mom and Dad since they left the day before yesterday. She figured they might be helping with the earthquake relief, but she has been worried they never even called to say they weren't coming. That isn't like them, even if they were out there somewhere trying to find us. We'd better call the resort and find out if Dad and Mom have been back there since they left the clinic."

Chad used the clinic phone to call the resort. This time he spoke in English, so even before he hung up, I'd gathered the resort hadn't seen Dr. and Mrs. M either—or Juvens.

Hanging up, Chad filled us in. "When none of us returned two days ago, the resort thought at first we must have flown back home without checking out properly. But when they discovered all our stuff was still in the bungalow, they got a little concerned. When I told him what happened to us and that Dad and Mom are still missing, they became a lot concerned. They're going to send a van to pick us up."

Chad went out to let the guard know a car would be coming for us. By the time he returned, Angelina had disappeared. She returned with bottles of water and a box of cookie wafers. I accepted my share gratefully, but I could barely choke down a swallow of water before a black tidal wave of worry overwhelmed me. I turned to Chad, who was placidly eating and drinking as though he'd relayed good news to us instead of more disaster.

Suddenly I let loose on Chad. "How can you sit here like things aren't as bad as ever? I was actually feeling hope when we got to the clinic because I thought this was all over and we were finally safe! Now all hope is gone! It was stupid to even think we were safe!"

"You are putting hope in people and circumstances, not God," Chad said firmly, though his expression was sympathetic. "God got us this far. So why not trust him for the rest?"

"Are you saying we shouldn't put any hope in people?" I put down my spoon. "I have to say I kind of agree since I've always figured Dr. and Mrs. M will get tired of us sooner or later and send us away."

Chad shook his head as though in disbelief. "You don't get it, Lexi! You and Levi were adopted into our family. That means forever—at least in the Michaels family. The day Dad met Levi for the first time in the ER, he came home and told us our family wasn't finished. He was sure God had chosen him to be yours and Levi's dad. Once he told Mom all about the two of you, she immediately started fixing up the spare bedroom for you, Lexi. And a bed in my room for Levi. She was so excited to finally be getting a daughter. And I was excited to get a brother and sister. Nothing's going to change. We're a family, period!"

I opened my mouth to say something, but Jen coughed. She had been staring at her half-empty water bottle, but she looked up as though she felt my gaze on her.

"You don't know how good you have it! To have parents who actually want you, I mean, and to be so sure you're meant to be their child. You think I'm a spoiled, pampered brat ..."

"You are!" Chad interrupted with a grin.

Jen shot him a hard look. "It's not as great as you'd think. Uncle David and my dad are brothers, but they are very different. My dad says Uncle David was offered a chance to be head of pediatrics at one of the most prestigious hospitals in the United States where he could be making tons of money. Instead he turned the offer down to do things like coming to Haiti every year. But it's more ... it's ..."

We waited for her to continue, but she shook her head.

"What, Jen?" Chad demanded. "You can't stop now! Spit it out!"

Hunching her shoulders, Jen finally went on. "Well, there are other differences too. I mean, I love my parents and all, but they're pretty demanding. I'm expected to know the proper thing to say when I meet the people my dad works with or when they host a fancy party. I'm expected to have perfect manners and be the perfect hostess alongside my mom. We don't do anything as a family just for fun. Everything is done for looks. Your parents aren't like them. They're for real. My parents would have a fit if they knew we boiled water to drink and duct taped my sandals."

"We had to do those things, Jen. And you were fine," I said.

Jen grimaced. "Inside I feel like a phony. I can't be who they want me to be, but I'm not like you guys either. I constantly worry about making a mistake and seeing my parents' disapproval. I've learned to hide my blunders while you guys admit yours and go on."

"That's what families do, Jen. Maybe you need to talk to your parents when we get home," Chad said.

"They wouldn't get it. It's sad."

Wow! I'd never thought I could feel sorry for Jen. I tried to think of something encouraging to say. But before anything came to mind, the nurse approached Chad and murmured a few soft Creole phrases.

He turned to us. "Our ride is here."

When we reached the gate, the guard had both sides opened wide, and a van emblazoned with the resort logo had pulled into the yard. The Haitian man standing beside the van was much younger than our last driver—no more than thirty—tall, and physically fit with a caramel complexion like Chad's and a prominent nose and jaw. I vaguely recognized him as someone I'd seen at the resort.

Still, I stopped a few feet away, and so did the others. After all, the last time we'd gotten into a van, we'd been kidnapped. Chad finally stepped forward to ask in English, "Do you have identification?"

Chapter Twenty-Three

"My name is Jean Pierre. We spoke on the phone earlier." The van driver's English was excellent. He pulled out his wallet and handed Chad what looked like a driver's license.

Chad checked the license, then turned to us. "This is the guy I talked to—Jean Pierre. He's with resort security." He turned back to the driver. "I didn't realize you were coming yourself to pick us up."

"With all that has happened and the continued absence of your parents, we wished to take every precaution."

Once I heard the man's voice, I remembered when I'd seen him before. He'd been among the security team that had questioned us after the burglary. We climbed into the van—Chad taking the front passenger seat—and Jean Pierre backed out of the gate.

We weren't far from the clinic before we began to see earthquake damage again—not just crumpled tin-roofed shacks and cracked cinderblock walls, but uprooted trees, landslides, and dirt-clogged streams. Several times the roads were blocked with debris, forcing Jean Pierre to turn around and go a different way.

I pulled out my iPad and snapped pictures—a woman with a basket balanced on her head and a toddler clinging to her skirt, making her way around a pile of debris—a group digging through the rubble of a collapsed building—a man and a young boy stacking broken bricks—two women ladling out something from a large kettle to a line of customers.

Before this trip, I didn't even know where Haiti was, much less the extent of the poverty. Yet the people were resilient. They were picking up and going on. I chose one of the pictures I'd taken and saved to my journal.

June 9
Haiti
Rich culture and tradition
Hemmed in poverty
Nature has dealt you a blow
How will you respond?
With resilience and confident hope?
With the will to go on?

I read my journal entry over again. Was I writing about them or me? I wasn't sure.

At least the earthquake didn't seem to have touched the capital city. We passed military convoys heading out of Port-au-Prince as well as trucks and white SUVs bearing the blue United Nations logo. Aid was on its way to the earthquake victims.

The van finally pulled up to the resort gate. Jean Pierre tapped his horn, and the gate swung open. The van drove in and on down the road, pulling up in front of our bungalow.

"I will be back with the police shortly to hear your account," Jean Pierre said as we climbed out of the van.

The van pulled away. Chad dug out a key and opened the front door of the bungalow. "I'm going to try calling Dad's cell phone again from the hotel phone."

As soon as we were inside, he headed over to the living room-kitchen area and grabbed the phone. He punched out numbers and waited, then punched again. Finally, he slammed down the phone. "It keeps going straight to voice mail."

"So, what next?" I asked.

Jen wrinkled her nose. "I don't know about you, but I'm going to shower and put on clean clothes. We've been in the same clothes for three days. I can't stand to smell myself, much less you guys!"

"And I'm going to call room service," Chad said. "We haven't had a real meal in three days either. What should we order, Levi?"

"Pizza?" Levi suggested.

"Well, we can try." Chad lifted the phone again as Jen hurried from the room.

I dropped to the sofa and stretched out. "Wake me when Jen's done."

I must have fallen sound asleep because when I awoke, the other three were sitting at the kitchen table around the remains of a pizza. A loud knock at the door awakened me.

As I struggled to a sitting position, Jen warned, "Don't open the door! We don't know who it is!"

Then we heard Jean Pierre's voice through the door. "Please open. I am here with the police."

Chad hurried to the door. For the next hour, Jean Pierre translated while we answered questions about the kidnapping, describing the kidnapper and his nephew, the house we'd been held in, the area, and everything we could remember. I played the video clip on my phone that had caught the kidnapper's face in the background.

Taking my phone, Jean Pierre texted a copy of the video to his own phone. "I'll forward a copy of this to hotel management as well as these officers."

"We still have no idea what happened to Juvens," Chad finished. "When we went to the room where we'd seen the kidnappers put him, it was empty. We were hoping he'd escaped, but I suppose he'd have been in touch with you all by now if he did."

"We'll find him," Jean Pierre said confidently. "And your parents. As for the four of you, we have contacted your embassy to explain your situation and ask for someone to come here and take charge until your parents have returned to you. Do you have family members you would also like to contact?"

"Yes, my parents," Jen spoke up. "They're somewhere in Europe on vacation. I'm not even sure where right now. But I can at least leave a voice mail to let them know what's going on." Sure enough, Jen's call reached only voice mail. She left a brief message, her voice commendably steady.

Shortly after, the police took their leave. Jean Pierre lingered to say, "Our security is on high alert, so I am confident you will be safe here. But you must not leave this bungalow without escort. I will contact you as soon as someone arrives from your embassy. Meanwhile ..." He nodded toward my cellphone. "... you have my number to which I texted your video. If there is anything you need, call me directly, and I will come immediately."

Once he was gone, Jen wailed, "Trust my parents not to be anywhere around when I need them! So now what do we do?"

"I don't know about you ..." I got back to my feet and reached for a slice of cold pizza, "... but I'm going to take a shower and eat, since the rest of you ate without me."

"We figured you needed the sleep as conked-out as you were," Chad said.

"Yes, and we did save you pizza," Levi added, looking worried.

I made myself smile at him. "Thanks."

"As to what next," Chad added, "since there is nothing else we really *can* do, we might as well try to get a full night's sleep. Who knows what tomorrow will bring."

As usual, Chad was right. By the time I'd devoured two pieces of cold pizza, showered, and changed, Jen was curled up in bed, fast asleep. Levi had waited up for me, so I went out to say goodnight, then headed to my own bed. By mutual decision, we'd left all the lights on in the living-room-kitchen area. After my catnap, I didn't expect to fall asleep easily, but weariness overwhelmed me, and I closed my eyes.

I was running down a dark mountain path. Footsteps pounded behind me. A roll of thunder sounded, and lightning split the sky. An ominous face glared at me. I screamed.

I sat up to find sunlight streaming into the room. From the neighboring bed, Jen was staring at me with sleep-heavy eyes. "You okay?"

I swallowed hard. "Yes, sorry. I dreamed I was running down a path in the dark and a hideous face appeared ahead of me."

"I'm surprised we didn't all have nightmares. The whole thing seems surreal now. I'm glad it's over." Rolling over, Jen closed her eyes. A moment later, a soft snore told me she'd gone back to sleep.

Sure, it's over for her! Her parents aren't still missing! I slid quietly out of bed. Emerging into the living-room, I heard gentle snoring from the couch. It was Chad. He must have gotten up in the night and fallen asleep there instead of going back to the room he and Levi shared.

I walked over to Dr. and Mrs. M's room and knocked softly. No answer. I grabbed the handle and opened the door, a lead feeling squeezing at my stomach. Sure enough, the room was empty with no sign they'd been home during the night.

A soft noise startled me. I spun around, hoping it was our parents, but worried it was someone else. It was just Chad, rubbing his sleepy eyes.

"Still not back?" he asked the obvious.

Next, Levi emerged from one bedroom and Jen from the other. "Are they back?" they chorused simultaneously.

"No, and nothing from the embassy either." Clenching my hands into fists, I looked over at Jen. "Maybe you're okay now, and the worst is over for you! But for Levi and me, it's back to foster care if Dr. and Mrs. M don't come back. I won't go. I can't do that again. Ever."

I felt ashamed the minute I saw the hurt expression on Chad's face and the bewildered one on Levi's. To my surprise, it was Jen who burst out in a huff, "You think we're not family? I know I said my parents aren't like Chad's are, but you really think my parents would let the foster system take their nephews and niece, the only cousins I've got?"

"Well, I assumed ..."

"Yeah, you did! But you assumed wrong. My parents might have thought Uncle David and Aunt Maggie were crazy to adopt you guys, but they would never turn you away. Like Chad said, 'You're family now.'"

Chad cleared his throat. "As touching as this is, we should call Jean Pierre and see if there's any news."

Just then, the phone rang. Chad reached for the receiver, saying, "He's probably calling right now."

"Here, let's put it on speaker so we can all hear." Jen punched the correct button as Chad put the receiver to his ear. But Jean Pierre's voice wasn't the one filling the room.

Chapter Twenty-Four

Chad broke into the flood of strongly accented English. "Juvens, what happened to you? We tried to find you, but you weren't in the room where they locked you up."

"Our captors moved me to a different location," Juvens responded. "I think they were afraid I would escape and help you if they left me close by. And I did escape, but I did not dare try to return to where they held you for fear they would take me prisoner again. Instead, I went directly to the clinic since I knew your parents would still be there until nightfall."

"Then you were the one who came and got Uncle David and Aunt Maggie!" Jen cut in. "We thought the kidnappers took them. So, where are they? Why aren't they back here?"

"That is why I am calling." Sadness and regret poured over the phone line as Juvens went on. "Your parents directed me to show them where you were being held. I advised them to call the police first, but they feared this might provoke our captors to harm you. I did as they asked and showed them the road. I drove with a gun at my side, but as I feared, the kidnappers were lying in wait. Now they have captured all three of us. They are threatening to kill all of us if you should call the police."

Jen let out a loud gasp as Juvens continued. "They have forced me to call you to say you must now pay a ransom for the release of your parents just as they required one for your own release."

"What kind of ransom?" I broke in angrily. "We're only teens. We don't have access to ransom!"

"You have access to drugs." My own gasp filled the air. "They know about the drugs your parents brought for the clinic. They say they will release your parents in exchange for those drugs."

Now I was really furious. "Sure they know about the drugs because the scumbag who kidnapped us tried to steal them once before already! But the drugs are at the clinic. We can't get them."

"You must get them from the clinic. If not, I fear greatly what these men will do to your parents. And to me."

I opened my mouth, but Chad put up a hand to hush me before speaking. "Those drugs are all needed at the clinic. People could die without those drugs. Even if we had access, there's no way we can do what you want."

"You have no choice if you want to see your parents again," Juvens said flatly.

Chad's face hardened, and his jaw clenched. But this time Jen was the one who broke in impatiently. "This is ridiculous! Those drugs were Uncle David's to begin with. He brought them to Haiti. If we have to use them for ransom, my parents will be happy to replace them. They can afford to do this, so what's the big deal?"

"Listen to the girl," Juvens's voice crackled on the speaker. "She speaks wisdom. Bring the drugs to Fort Jacques tonight. Do not come until it is dark. And do not say anything of this to the police. You must come alone, or they will kill your parents—and me as well. They will be watching. They have eyes and ears everywhere!"

The line went dead. Jen swung around on the rest of us. "Okay, I guess we'd better go to the clinic and get those drugs."

I stared at her incredulously. "Are you kidding? You think we can just walk in and ask for them?"

"No, we can't just ask for them," Chad said. "They'd ask why, and when they found out, they'd call the police—exactly what

Juvens warned us not to do. We'll find another way."

Now I stared at Chad. "You're the last person I thought would be encouraging her. We should be calling the police, security, the embassy, someone. Not planning a drug deal like some dumb movie. We're teens, not action heroes!"

Chad shook his head. "I don't agree. One, kidnappers trade hostages for ransom all the time here—like a business—and hurting hostages isn't going to convince the next victims to pay up. They have no reason not to let Mom and Dad go if they get what they're after. Two ..."

"Two?" I said impatiently as he paused. He didn't answer, instead he strode over into Mom and Dad's bedroom. I trailed him as he began digging through drawers, then pulled out suitcases and opened them.

"And?" Jen said. She and Levi had followed us into the bedroom.

Chad threw down the last suitcase he was rifling through. "Two, I have an idea how to get the drugs and get them to the fort, but we need cash since we can hardly ask Jean Pierre to drive us. And Stevens got all of ours, so I was hoping maybe Mom and Dad had spare change stashed somewhere."

Jen crossed her arms as Chad's gaze moved to her. "Well, I sure don't have any! I had all my cash in my bag. He even took my credit card." She turned to me. "What about yours?"

"No, he didn't get mine, since I've never had a credit card," I said with sarcasm. "And neither has Levi."

"Maybe this will help." I hadn't noticed Levi leave the room, so I was startled when he stepped through the door and held out a roll of cash.

"Where'd you get that?" Jen demanded, snatching the roll from his hand.

"Under my mattress," Levi answered simply.

I might have known. Every time we got a bit of money, Levi

stashed most of it away in case some dire emergency cropped up—like running away from an abusive foster home. Even with Dr. and Mrs. M, he still didn't feel secure enough to not need his getaway stash.

Chad lifted the roll from Jen's palm and counted it. "Over a hundred dollars. This will be plenty. Taxis and stores are happy to take American dollars, even if they usually sock you in the exchange rate. Thanks, Levi. You saved us on this."

"So what now?" Jen asked.

"Well, I was thinking the guard might help us if I explain what happened. He's been there since I was little, and Dad helped his grandkids when they were really sick. I think he'll want to help Mom and Dad. And he's got keys to get us in and out unseen. Then it's a quick trip to the fort, and this will all be over."

Over? I no longer trusted Chad's optimism, but I couldn't think of a better plan, so I followed Chad's instructions, stuffing our backpacks with extra water and snacks as well as anything useful we could think of, including steak knives from the kitchen. Jen had changed from her sandals—one of several spare $100 sandals—to sneakers like the rest of us. Chad, of course, didn't have a backpack, but he emptied out the duffle-bag in which he'd brought clothes.

"To hold the drugs," he answered my curious glance.

Locking up the bungalow, we made our way to the resort gate, doing our best to look like tourists headed for the beach or shopping. I was worried Jean Pierre might have given orders restricting us to the property until the embassy person showed up. But though the front guard gave us a sharp glance, he didn't hesitate to open the gate.

Once we were out on the street, Chad flagged down a taxi, and we were on our way. Dread and adrenaline tangoed within me. The next few hours were crucial, and I didn't know how to deal with all the emotions flooding my mind.

The drive to the clinic was about an hour, and the roads were even more congested with army and relief convoys than the day before. There were now streams of people on foot as well, all heading for the city. From the awkward bundles they carried, I guessed they were earthquake victims whose homes had been destroyed.

Finally, the taxi pulled up to the clinic gate. As we climbed out, Chad went around to the driver's window, speaking to him in Creole and handing him a few bills. Tucking the bills away, the driver leaned back and crossed his arms behind his head.

"What did you say?" Jen demanded.

"I asked him to wait for us. Told him we'd pay him extra if he takes us to one more stop, then back to the resort."

Chad knocked on the gate. The elderly guard, Samuel, peered through the narrow slit in the pedestrian gate, then swung it open. As soon as we were inside and the gate shut, Chad began talking to Samuel in a flood of Creole. If the rest of us couldn't understand a word, I could guess the content as the guard's face went through a succession of expressions from surprise to anger to nodding agreement.

Chad broke off and turned to me. "Hey, Lexi, I thought of something. Did you bring your iPad? I want to show Samuel the video. After all, the kidnapper said something about holding a grudge against Mom and Dad. About the only place they've been in Haiti is the clinic, so maybe the kidnapper had something to do with the clinic. If he did, Samuel here might recognize him."

I dug my iPad from my backpack, pulled up the video, and handed it to Chad. Chad in turn placed the iPad in Samuel's gnarled hands, hit play, and leaned in close to point out the scarred man in the background.

The guard's loud gasp was my only warning as he dropped

the iPad. I managed to catch it before it hit the ground. The old man was now backing away from us, shaking his head violently as he addressed a stream of frightened Creole at Chad.

"What's the matter?" Jen demanded. "Did he recognize the kidnapper?"

Chad turned toward us, his usually cheerful expression discouraged. "He recognizes him all right. And now he says he can't help us after all. He says the scarred man in the video is pure evil, and if he helps us, the man will surely find out and come after him too—and his family."

Chapter Twenty-Five

"What do you mean?" Jen demanded impatiently. "Who is the guy? Why is the old man so afraid of him?"

Chad didn't answer. By this time, he and the guard were engaged in another heated conversation. I was as impatient as Jen but there was no point in interrupting.

Finally, Chad turned to us. "Samuel says the man who kidnapped us is named Frantz Damis. A long time ago, he worked for the clinic as their driver. But he got caught stealing drugs and arrested. He ended up in jail. Samuel didn't know he'd been released."

"Do you believe him?" Jen demanded skeptically. "How do we know he isn't in cahoots with this Frantz?"

Chad gave his cousin a frown. "Yes, I do believe him, especially since he admits to helping Frantz steal the drugs all those years back. Frantz knew Samuel had once stolen medicine for his very sick grandchild, so Frantz was blackmailing him to get access to the pharmacy. Samuel didn't have to admit what he's done, so I believe the rest too."

"But what does it have to do with Dr. and Mrs. M?" I asked. "Why would the kidnapper want revenge on them because this Frantz got arrested for stealing drugs?"

"Well, it's simple. He blames Mom and Dad for his arrest. It seems Samuel here was feeling worse and worse about helping Frantz steal, so he finally told Dad about the thefts and the blackmail. Then he helped Dad set up a trap, so when Frantz came back one last time to steal drugs, the police had the place staked out."

"And you believe all this?" Jen demanded even more skeptically. "For all you know, the old man made up the whole story to get us to trust him and has been working with the kidnapper all these years."

"I believe him because I was here— our first visit after I was adopted," Chad said calmly. "I'd forgotten all about it, but I remember the flashing lights and sirens when the police raided the clinic. It was nighttime, and I was standing right over there on the guesthouse verandah with Mom and Dad."

Chad gestured to a small building nestled in the shade of citrus and mango trees in the right rear section of the compound. "That's where we usually stay when we come. I didn't know then, but they were arresting Frantz. I do remember the huge load of drugs we brought on the trip for the clinic. And if the guy's been in a Haitian jail for the last ten years, I can see why he'd want revenge. You can't imagine how awful those places are."

Jen, Levi, and I were now all staring at Chad with mouths hanging open. It all sounded like a farfetched movie plot. But then a whole lot of our time in Haiti had felt that way!

"The question is whether Samuel's going to help us," I said. "Surely he can see the best way to protect his family is to help us get Mom and Dad back and get Frantz back into jail. I mean, if Frantz knows Samuel helped in his arrest, then he'll be after him next."

"I agree," Chad said. "Now let me see if I can convince Samuel."

The following discussion involved lots of passionate Creole from Chad and frantic protests from Samuel. But at last the old man hunched his shoulders and started limping across the courtyard.

Chad turned to the rest of us. "He's agreed to help us get the drugs to trade for our parents. I promised we'd keep his name out of it."

Levi, Jen, and I followed Chad and Samuel to a cinder-block building opposite the guesthouse at the rear of the compound. Though there was no one else around, the elderly guard glanced around furtively before opening the door. Stepping inside, I saw what looked like a doctor's examining room with a pair of elevated cots, shelves, and a sink, but little of the more modern equipment Dr. M had in his office back home.

The guard limped on past to a door at the far-right end of the room. He inserted another key and pushed the door open. Levi, Jen, and I waited outside while Chad and the guard went in. I could hear them murmuring in Creole. I decided I would learn basic phrases before we come back next year. I corrected myself—if we come back.

The passage of time while we waited for Chad and the guard to return seemed far longer than a few minutes. Chad's duffel bag was now bulging. My body was stiff from tensing up at every sound. Surely someone was going to burst in demanding to know what we were doing.

"Did you get what they asked for?" I asked tensely.

Chad nodded. "This is most of what Mom and Dad brought in their luggage, but I did leave a bit of each drug in case of emergency here. The kidnappers won't know the difference."

The courtyard was still empty as we headed back to the gate. I heard a woman's voice singing in warm, rich tones through the bars of an open window. The words were in French, but the tune was a hymn I'd heard often at the Michaels's church. "Great is Thy faithfulness, O God, my Father." The clinic administrator must be busy with the patients. We were actually going to get away with this!

Samuel seemed less sure. His hands shook as he unlocked the gate, and his wrinkled, old face looked unhappy. He muttered something as Levi helped Chad carry out the duffel bag. As soon as we were all out, he slammed the gate, and we heard the key turn in the lock.

"What did he say?" Jen asked.

"He said to watch out for Frantz," Chad responded. "He is as trustworthy as a snake."

The taxi was still pulled up outside the gate, but the driver's face was filled with impatience. He hurried around to the trunk so Chad could add the duffel bag to the backpacks already stashed there, showing no interest in it. As we climbed in, Chad handed over a wad of American dollars. This seemed to cheer the driver, and we were quickly on our way again.

Chad sat next to the driver; the rest of us were shoulder to shoulder in the back seat. My heart rate accelerated, pulse pounding in my throat, as we jolted past a dusty, maroon four-door sedan heading for the clinic. Were our kidnappers returning?

But the cloud of dust we'd kicked up was too great to see the other vehicle's driver, and I reminded myself this was a main road for Haiti, dirty and winding though it might be. Of course, we'd be passing other cars.

My stomach twisted again as we bounced along the narrow mountain road, taking one unmarked turn after another, occasionally inching around debris from the earthquake. How could we even be sure the driver was actually taking us to the fort, as promised? Maybe this was another hostage situation such as had gotten us in trouble in the first place.

Still, Chad seemed confident we were headed the right direction. And unlike our prior kidnappers, we were four against a clearly unarmed driver. I tried to relax, but it seemed ages before we found ourselves on house-lined dirt streets. There was more traffic here as well, including plenty of dirty four-door sedans, I reminded myself.

You've got to calm down if you're going to get through this! I told myself sternly. Besides, the kidnappers are up ahead waiting, not following us.

The taxi finally pulled into a parking lot fronted by thick trees. High above them, I caught a glimpse of gray stone that must be Fort Jacques. The parking lot was reasonably full, and visitors were wandering down through a trail on the far side of where we parked.

"We'll have to hike the rest of the way on foot," Chad said as he climbed out of the car. The driver got out too, walking around to open the trunk. Levi, Jen, and I shouldered our backpacks while Chad hefted the duffle-bag to one shoulder as though it weighed less than my own pack. Chad engaged the driver in conversation, then handed him another wad of dollars. The driver climbed back into the taxi.

"Hey, where's he going?" Jen demanded as the taxi backed out. "Isn't he going to wait for us?

"No, I told him we'd find our own way back," Chad said. "Since the fort shuts at dark, I don't want him getting curious as to why we're staying so late. We can always walk into town from here and catch another taxi."

Following Chad across the parking lot, we started up the trail. It led up through more dense forest. As we climbed, several dozen hikers passed us heading down. The time must be later than I'd realized if tourists were already leaving the fort.

We eventually emerged onto a flattish plateau filled with mossy-gray fortifications. They resembled a run-down, crumbling version of the old Spanish coastal fort outside of St. Augustine, Florida. I guess one colonial stone fort was much like another.

By the time we reached the top, where the view offered a spectacular panorama of Port au Prince and the harbor beyond, the sun was dropping behind the mountains. I'd grown accustomed to the short twilights this close to the equator, where the sky went from sunset to full dark within an hour of the sun's disappearance. And I could see why tourists were abandoning the place as there was no evidence of electricity or any modern additions to the site. Not even a tour guide was anywhere in sight. The only entrance into the fort itself—a high, arched, wooden double gate—was locked and barred.

"So what do we do now?" Jen asked gloomily. "Juvens never said what to do after we got here or how he would find us."

"We wait." Chad lowered the duffle-bag to the ground. "They probably have someone posted to watch for us. But they aren't going to show themselves until dark. We might as well have something to eat. It's been a long time since breakfast."

It felt surreal to be sitting at the edge of a high look-out, munching on granola bars and swigging bottled water. We watched the sunset fade over the distant ocean as though this were merely another holiday outing. As darkness fell, our surroundings grew spooky. Quite some time had passed since we'd seen or heard another human being. Even the birds seemed to have gone to sleep. Then we heard rustles in the underbrush. I jumped at a snapped twig.

"Turn on a light!" Jen demanded in a loud whisper. "Who's got the flashlight?"

"No, we don't want to draw attention," Chad whispered back. "The kidnappers might not be the only ones who'd see it. Let's at least give them time to make the first move."

The darkness deepened. There wasn't even more than a sliver of moon, and the distant pool of light that was Port au Prince didn't cast even a shadow up here on the heights of Fort Jacque. I heard another twig snap and had to clap my hand over my mouth to stop a scream.

"I can't take any more of this!" Jen hissed.

"Shhh!" Chad and Levi hissed back together.

Just then a star pierced the darkness. No, not a star—a flashlight beam. It moved back and forth across the gravel of the lookout. Then the beam tilted upwards to illuminate a man's face.

It was Juvens!

Chapter Twenty-Six

"Do you have the drugs?" Juvens asked tensely.

Chad lifted the duffle-bag in answer.

"Good. Then follow me."

We made our way along the high bulk of a stone wall, the dirt path illuminated only by Juvens's flashlight. The path rounded the corner. Up ahead, the flashlight beam danced across the arched entrance gate.

"We can't get in there," Chad spoke up. "It's locked."

"Not any longer." Juvens was already tugging open the heavy wooden panel. "This is the way to your parents."

Now I knew how the kidnappers had managed to hold hostages at a tourist attraction. Frantz must have paid off someone here as he had the watchman at the clinic.

"What about Frantz and his nephew?" Jen demanded. "Where are they?"

"Frantz!" Juvens suddenly swung around, his flashlight beam probing our faces. "Where do you come by that name?"

Jen's eyebrows rose in the light of the flashlight beam. "You mean it isn't the name of the kidnapper?"

"Yes, perhaps, but ... well, it seems you have a story of your own to tell. It matters not. Hurry! Those holding your parents are not patient."

The wind gusted as we followed Juvens across a cobble-stone courtyard. I rubbed my arms for warmth. As though he'd read my thoughts, Levi stepped up beside me, tugging a sweatshirt from his backpack and pushing it into my hands. I pulled it on, grateful for the warmth—and his thoughtfulness. Levi's gesture was a welcome reminder that he always had my back as much as I had his.

Levi stayed close beside me as we picked our way through the fort's interior. Parts of the outer wall had crumbled, and we had to keep stepping around debris. Either my eyes were adjusting to the darkness or the stars were getting brighter as their faint illumination now allowed me to get a sense of our surroundings.

The fort loomed over us, casting an eerie shadow, large and foreboding. The structure was massive, resembling the front of a ship, but a large crack had split it in two. A row of cannons stood like sentinels along the top. We descended a stone staircase, then skirted a large square filled with dark, rippling liquid.

"Is that a pool?" I whispered to Chad.

"It's rain storage," Chad whispered back. "The pool is a good twenty feet deep, so be careful not to fall in."

Ahead, a dark hole in the fort wall became another staircase, narrow and steep, descending into what looked like an underground tunnel. I stopped short as Juvens gestured for us to enter. "What's down there?"

"The dungeons?" Jen added, her voice quavering as she pressed closer to me.

"It is where your parents are waiting for you," Juvens responded impatiently. "Come!"

Suddenly Chad planted his solid bulk at the top of the stairs. "No, we're not going down there. We're certainly not going to let Frantz corral us underground, so he has all of us instead of just my parents. You said Frantz agreed to trade our parents for the drugs. We did our part. So now we'll stay right here with the drugs while you go tell Frantz to bring our parents up. He gets the drugs once we get our parents."

Even in the scanty light, I could see a furious expression cross Juvens's face, replaced immediately by an ingratiating smile. "That will not work. I have already told Frantz I will bring you down to your parents."

"Well, tough!" Chad snapped back. "There's four of us and one of you. And you are not getting us down those stairs. Like we'd trust Frantz to let us back up. We'll stay hidden out of sight back there while you go let him know we're ready to trade."

"But there is not just one." A voice came out of the dark. "There are two."

Jen let out a screech as another flashlight beam sprang to life. Okay, maybe I screeched too. Above the beam was the sneering face of the younger kidnapper, Stevens. Below the beam, a gun was pointed at us.

He grinned. "You give me the drugs. Then I show you where Frantz is."

Chad was already lowering the duffle-bag from his shoulder. I swallowed back sick dismay as he swung it towards Frantz's nephew. Then I caught the grim clenching of Chad's jaw—just before he lunged forward after the duffel bag.

The force of the duffel bag caught Stevens smack in the torso. The gun went flying. Already, Levi was joining Chad in wrestling the younger kidnapper to the ground. I looked around for the gun, spotting it a few feet from Juvens. The resort driver leaned down and scooped it up as Chad and Levi twisted both of Stevens's arms behind his back and pushed him face first into the cobblestones.

I let out my relief in a big whoosh. "Great! Now we have the gun, and we're down to dealing with Frantz. With Stevens as hostage, we can trade him for Dr. and Mrs. M without giving up the drugs."

But the gun was once again up, pointing in our direction. Only this time it was Juvens's steady hand pointing the gun at us. I froze, stunned. "Juvens, what are you doing?"

"What does it look like?" The resort driver waved the gun toward Stevens. "Let him go!"

When Chad and Levi didn't move, Juvens shifted the gun barrel toward Jen and me. "Now, or you can take your pick which of these I shoot first."

Chad and Levi slowly released Stevens and got to their feet. Levi's face was expressionless, but Chad's was a mask of shock at being betrayed. Scrambling to his feet, Stevens snatched up the duffel bag of drugs.

"Like I said—two of us!" he sneered. "Me and Cousin Juvens. He works at the resort for Frantz."

I couldn't believe my ears—or my eyes. All pretense of regret or friendliness had evaporated from Juvens's face. He looked us over like a shark measuring the plumpness of the tuna he was considering for dinner.

Beside me, Jen burst out angrily. "How could you do this to us? I thought you were our friend and you were helping us! Then you're the one who arranged the kidnapping while you were pretending to be kidnapped too?"

Juvens raised his shoulders in a shrug. "You Americans are so easy to fool. You think everyone is your friend. Now, enough talk. Frantz is still waiting, and unlike me, he has little patience."

Chad's jaw was still tensed, his hands balled into fists. For a moment, I was afraid he was going to resist. Then he followed Stevens down the stairs, jaw set. Jen, Levi, and I followed in single file, with Juvens and his gun bringing up the rear.

The stairs were stone, built against the wall on one side with the other side open. Slick green mold covered part of them while other parts had crumbled. A single wrong step, and I could fall off the edge, plummeting to the dark depths below. Sucking in a breath, I pressed as close to the wall as I could.

Why wasn't there a handrail?

Halfway down, loose rocks shifted under my feet and toppled down the steps. I froze. Immediately Levi stepped up beside me, perilously close to the edge himself, and took my hand.

"It's okay. We're almost there," he whispered. "Step when I do."

I did, and we quickly reached the bottom. I took a deep breath and blew it out, then directed a grateful smile to my twin.

Stevens led us down the tunnel, then turned left. Several antique-looking wooden doors lined this new passage. Were our parents behind one of them? Would we soon be joining them?

A noise to my right startled me. I spun around, only to see an archway leading away into darkness. I wasn't the only one who heard something. Stevens immediately pushed through to shine his flashlight down the tunnel. The beam caught at a small pair of eyes close to the ground.

Stevens lowered his flashlight and called a Creole phrase back to Juvens at the rear. I understood the Creole word for rat. I wasn't so sure what noise I'd heard. I could have sworn I'd glimpsed a much larger, darker shape back in the tunnel.

Or maybe Frantz had other guards posted around the fort—perhaps whoever had provided the key to the interior of the fort.

We passed several heavy wooden doors before reaching one secured with a shiny, new steel padlock. A tiny, rectangular window in the door at the height of a man's eyes had rusting bars too close together to insert more than a hand between them. Stevens inserted a key in the padlock. Pulling it loose, he tugged open the door and motioned for us to enter.

"The dungeon," he said nastily, "where the blancs once imprisoned my people. Now it is the blancs who do not leave here until they provide what we ask."

Did he mean we weren't the first foreigners held for ransom here? There was no light beyond the door, and the air emerging smelled dank like the interior of a cave. None of us moved to be the first to enter. Tears of despair stung my eyes. Where were Dr. and Mrs. M? Had Juvens lied about them too?

Were they even still alive?

Chapter Twenty-Seven

"Enter quickly!" Juvens called from the rear. "Or I will shoot!"

Chad stepped in first, Jen at his heels. I felt Levi's hand slip into mine for moral support as we followed. The door slammed shut, and we heard the click of the padlock snapping back into place, leaving us in dank, cold blackness.

Then Levi pulled his hand from mine, and a moment later the most welcome radiance dispelled the darkness. He had dug out a flashlight. At least they hadn't taken away our backpacks this time—maybe because they knew there was nothing in them to help us escape. The beam swept around, illuminating a large brick and concrete room that indeed looked like a cave with no windows. The only entrance was a heavy, padlocked door. Green mold grew all over the walls, and moisture dripped from the ceiling, leaving the floor slimy underfoot.

Then, as Levi's flashlight probed the rear of the room, I gasped. Dr. and Mrs. M were seated against the back wall, hands and feet bound, and their mouths gagged. I rushed forward.

"Dad! Mom!" The words burst out naturally. I tugged at the gag on my mom's mouth, but it was knotted too tightly. Then Levi and Chad were both beside me, the penknives they'd purchased at the mission already open. They sliced away the gags, then sawed at the ropes.

The instant the ropes fell away, Dad and Mom were on their feet, pulling all of us into a group hug. But the hugs were brief, and Dad and Mom stepped away, wearing similar worried frowns on their faces.

"What are you doing here?" Mom asked. "We hoped you returned to the resort when we found out you had escaped."

"Yes," Dad added heavily. "Whatever happens to Mom and me, we'd taken heart, believing at least you were free and out of harm's way. Especially since Frantz and his associates clearly had no idea where you were. How did they find you again?"

Chad grimaced. "My fault, Dad. I'm the one who trusted Juvens when he said he could help us free you in exchange for the drugs we brought from the states."

"The drugs!" Mom exclaimed. "So that's what they were after! I wondered why they weren't pushing for a cash ransom. But what is this about Juvens? We thought he'd been captured along with us when he took us to where you'd been held. He seemed such a nice man, really concerned about you kids."

So we weren't the only ones who'd been fooled by Juvens. I shouldn't have felt any better in this awful place, but I did. Or maybe it was being all together again as a family—even though we were all locked up.

"It wasn't your fault, Chad," Dad said. "We were all fooled. And I should have thought of Frantz, but I assumed he was still in prison."

"The prison where you caused me to be all those years."

The dungeon door had swung open. Frantz stood in the doorway, holding up a large fluorescent lantern. I would have been tempted to rush him if not for the gun he held in his other hand. The tensing of Chad's tall body beside me told me he had the same thought.

The light blinded my eyes as he lifted the lantern higher. "Ah. What a happy family reunion."

Chad stepped into the fluorescent beam, his fists balled. "We brought you what you wanted. You promised you'd free our parents if we paid the ransom."

Frantz's cruel laughter filled the night. "Yes, it is true for other foolish tourists the fort custodian allows us to keep here from time to time. But you are different. The doctor here cost me ten years of my life. And in such a place!"

Frantz's shudder was genuine as he dropped his voice to a whisper. "You complain of these accommodations? You cannot dream of what prison is like for a prisoner with no money to bribe the guards. The beatings of the guards. The rats. Enough rotted food and filthy water only to stay alive."

The grin spread across his face, making him look crazed. "Now I will let you, Dr. Michaels, know what I suffered all these years. And you will have the pleasure of watching your wife and children suffer too. Where is the God you speak so much of now, doctor? Believe me, you will not find him here in the darkness once I take away all you possess, including your flashlight my careless nephew and cousin have allowed your children to retain."

Dad stepped in front of Chad and stretched his arms wide, projecting a protective presence like a solid rock. Maybe it was silly of me, but I felt suddenly safer sheltered behind his strong figure.

"God is still with us, here as everywhere, in the darkness as in the light, as he has always been. You cannot take our one hope away from us."

"We will see if you still believe such in a few days. Stevens! Juvens!"

There was no response, but a swift movement from the dark doorway behind Frantz caught my eye. Was it the same dark shape I had glimpsed in the tunnel? What looked like an arm rose above Frantz's head, and a sudden suspicion crossed my mind.

"Where are those two? They were to store the drugs and bring bindings for the rest of you. If they were not family, I would fire them."

Frantz began to turn toward the door. As he did, I saw Chad tense, lowering his head as I'd seen him do when tackling an opponent on the football field. Did he think he could charge Frantz and get the gun? He was certain to be killed. I could not let Frantz complete the turn.

Clutching at my stomach, I let out a low groan. It had to be the oldest trick in the book, but I couldn't think of anything else. It worked. Frantz swiveled back in my direction.

Dad glanced back at me. "Are you okay, Lexi?"

"My stomach. I think it's all the stress and fear getting to me." I was keeping an eye on the dark arch of the doorway. Then it happened. The raised shadow came down—right on Frantz's head. The kidnapper stumbled forward. The gun went flying, and Chad dived for it.

Rolling smoothly back to his feet, he grinned widely at all of us, but his words were for me. "Didn't I tell you God would rescue us one way or another? Never lose hope ... right, Lexi?"

"I have never been called God before."

I recognized the amused voice even before the tall shape stepped forward into the circle of light created by the lantern. Frantz lay beside the lantern, appearing to be unconscious.

"Jean-Pierre!" Jen exclaimed. "What are you doing here?"

"I thought it might be you!" I put in. "Or at least I hoped so!"

Jen turned and stared at me. "What do you mean? How could you possibly have known! You're making it up."

"No, I'm not!" I answered back. "I kept thinking someone might be following us. First a maroon car. Then sounds like footsteps and a shadow. At first, I thought it was someone working with the kidnappers. But since no one ever showed up, I thought—I hoped—maybe it was someone trying to hide from the kidnappers. Maybe even help us. And the only one I could think of who might try or have any idea we were in trouble was

Jean Pierre. When I saw him in the doorway, I knew it had to be him."

"So that's why you pretended to be sick." Jen looked impressed. "To distract Frantz. Not a bad move."

"You were right—I was following you." Jean Pierre paused to pull a pair of large zip-ties from his pocket. Bending forward, he zip-tied Frantz's hands behind his back, then the kidnapper's ankles. Frantz was now moaning, so he must not have been too badly hurt.

Straightening, Jean Pierre nodded at the kidnapper. "I ran the image you gave me through Interpol and identified the man as a Frantz Damis, who had recently been released from prison after a ten-year sentence for drug dealing. The report indicated a connection to the clinic where Dr. Michaels worked and a reason Frantz might desire revenge. More pertinently, the report listed family members, including a Juvens who has been working at the resort since long before my time—the same who was supposedly kidnapped along with you kids.

"This information sent me looking for you, only to find you'd left the resort. Our data base revealed you'd recently received a call through the resort phone system from a cell phone registered to Juvens. By now, I had a good idea he wasn't the kidnap victim as we thought. I headed to the clinic, hoping it might be where you'd gone. I spotted the bunch of you leaving the clinic in a taxi, so I followed, which led me here.

"I waited and watched until I saw Juvens approach you. I do apologize for letting Juvens get the jump on you. I had moved out of earshot to call the authorities and let them know to move in."

"The authorities?" Dad interrupted. Then noise broke out in the passageway. I tensed as half-a-dozen men in police uniforms pushed two men ahead of them into the dungeon—Juvens and Stevens, both with their hands zip-tied behind them.

"Yes, I had relayed my suspicions earlier, but they had not yet reached the fort." Jean Pierre turned to say something in French to the police, then nodded toward their captives. "I was able to—how do you say it in America?—'take down' these two when they separated from Frantz and went to the storage room where they have their quarters. Then the authorities arrived."

He gestured to the men in police uniform. "Unfortunately, the gun had been passed over to Frantz here, so we dared not attack openly for fear he might begin shooting. It was my hope we could sneak up unheard, and so it happened."

He nudged Frantz before glancing approvingly at Chad, who was still holding the gun. "Thankfully, this young man capably dealt with my last concern."

Stepping forward, he lifted the gun from Chad's hand. Jen's mouth was gaping as she looked from Chad to Jean Pierre to the crowded doorway.

"Wow!" she exclaimed. "Are you some kind of ninja or Special Forces?"

Jean Pierre grinned at her. "I was in the military special unit and then the police force before I became head of security. I was hired for those skills. Keeping our guests safe is a high priority. And now, are you all ready to return home? Or at least to the resort for what is left of this night?"

"More than ready!" I said.

Juvens and Stevens had by now been shoved down to sit next to Frantz. None of us got too close as we filed out past them. I paused in the doorway to pull my iPad from my backpack. "One last photo for my vacation album."

I carefully framed Frantz, Juvens, and Stevens— now with zip-tied hands and feet, their expressions glaring hatred—and snapped the photo. Then I followed my family down the passageway and up the crumbled stone staircase to the fresh air of freedom.

Chapter Twenty-Eight

We had to scramble down the dark path to the parking lot. Two police vehicles, a police van, and the dusty maroon sedan Jean Pierre had used to tail us were the only vehicles parked at this hour. We all squeezed into the police van for the drive back to the resort with Jean Pierre leading the way in his sedan.

Once we'd been dropped off at our bungalow, there was another flurry of activity as we explained everything to the security team, giving our own reports in detail to a police sergeant, and calling the American embassy, as well as Jen's parents. We also thanked Jean Pierre for rescuing us so many times he was beginning to look embarrassed. Finally, he and all the others left.

It was after midnight by now, and Mom tried to get us all to go to bed, but no one was willing to go to their separate bedrooms. Instead, we all curled up on the couch and chairs in the family room. Dad looked around at all of us, his expression serious.

"Kids, I think it's time to go home. This wasn't at all the vacation I'd planned for you."

"I don't want to go home," Chad protested. "I want to help at the clinic. There will be more to do there with the earthquake casualties."

Dad shook his head. "I love your compassion and your desire to help, but the clinic is not the place for any of you. We need trained medical personnel for most of the tasks."

"We could play with the children whose parents are being

treated," Chad suggested. "I've done that before."

"Maybe," Dad agreed. "But the whole point of this vacation was for you teens to get to know each other better."

I looked at Chad, Jen, and Levi, then smiled. "We did exactly that. We got to know each other better than we ever would have here at the resort. We worked together to escape from the kidnappers, survived hiking through the mountains, and got pitched into a river."

"It all sounds pretty intriguing," Mom agreed. "Why don't you start at the beginning and tell us everything that happened?"

We took turns filling in all the details. Mom and Dad looked horrified by the time we told of our escape through the woods, the collapsing bridge, the trip downriver, and especially our escapades stealing the drugs and delivering them to the fort. Thankfully, the police had already turned the drugs back over for Mom and Dad to return to the clinic.

Then Dad and Mom told us their own story of how Juvens had come to the clinic, pretending to help them rescue us. We already knew some of the details of their own capture, being tied up in the fort, hoping Juvens had gotten away to warn us, then their dismay when we in turn were pushed into the dungeon. We all listened and exclaimed over each other's stories.

By the time we'd all finished, everyone was finally ready for sleep, but Chad, Levi, Jen, and I still didn't want to separate, so we pulled our mattresses out into the living-room and flopped down like a big slumber party.

Though I'd only been asleep a few hours, I woke up with the first light of dawn creeping under the blinds. A quick glance told me the others were still asleep. Slipping noiselessly into the bedroom Jen and I had shared, I changed into clean shorts and a T-shirt, grabbed my iPad, then headed to the beach.

Turquoise waves lapped at my feet. I strolled across the cool, moist sand to the cove where Dad and I had seen the sand dollar. I set my iPad on my towel, well away from the water. I had too many photos on it from this trip to risk getting it wet.

I sat down at the edge of the surf, gazing out over the sea where orange and pink was beginning to stain the horizon. The events of the past few days replayed over and over in my mind. In a way it seemed like a distant dream. In other ways, it was all too real. Overall, it had been horrible, yet we'd come through it.

I sensed someone behind me and turned. Dad stood a few feet away, watching me. He smiled. "Did you figure it out?"

"Figure it out?" I repeated.

He sat down on the sand beside me. "What you're looking for. What was missing."

I nodded, remembering now our first conversation right on this spot. "Yes. It was hope. Hope was missing from my life."

"Hope?"

"Yes. I hoped you would be my dad forever and I'd found my forever home. Hope there would be a happily ever after for me."

Dad put an arm around my shoulder and gave me a squeeze. "There is a happily ever after for you, Lexi, but first you need to look to God for what you seek. I will always love you as my daughter, but God's love is stronger. And he is the source of hope."

We sat side by side, watching the waves for a long moment before I responded. "Chad told me God gives us confident hope, and it leads to peace and joy."

"And he's right. Hey, look!" Dad pointed to the shoreline where a speck of white was being pulled back and forth in the surf.

I walked over to it and squatted. I reached into the waves, allowing the sand dollar to wash onto my hand.

June 11
Sitting side by side
Turquoise waves rush to meet us
Father and daughter forever
Reaching out for what's within my grasp
A perfect sand dollar washes into my hand
Catching life
Catching hope
Joy
Peace

About the author:

Kathy grew up in northern Indiana, lived in three different continents while her husband was in the USAF, and now lives in the Florida Panhandle. She and her husband have eight children, five of whom are adopted, three from Haiti and two from the United States. They also have six grandchildren. Kathy's favorite activities are those that involve traveling and adventures that include her children and grandchildren.

In order to better relate to the characters in her stories, Kathy has done things such as whitewater rafting, certify in scuba diving, and get her motorcycle endorsement. She draws the line at sky diving.

Chapter One

Night is my favorite time of day. Night's when I can be anonymous, swallowed by darkness, when I run to outdistance the voices in my head and the images that are never far away.

As I stretch out on my quilt-covered bed, memories haunt me. I can't shut them off. I text my best friend Thorn, a high school freshman like me. Then, as I've done so many nights, I swing a leg, then the other, over my windowsill and slide onto the porch roof, careful to avoid the places that need repair. The noxious smell of the paper mill three miles away assaults my nose. It's stronger than usual tonight.

It's mid-February, and, while it's not cold in the Florida Panhandle, the air is a bit chilly now the sun's gone down. A breeze blows a wisp of thick, dark hair into my face. I brush it aside and stride to the roof's edge, jump, and front-flip midair. Landing in a crouch, I roll to break my fall. It's no problem for me. Just another bit of freerunning. And that's what I do best.

I pull my phone from my pocket and text: "Meet me at the playground."

My phone buzzes, and I read the one-word answer. "Now?"

"It's important."

Almost instantly, the phone vibrates again. "On my way."

I stick my phone in my pocket, then jog down the street to the elementary school playground where I first saw freerunning in action—a group of older boys racing around the playground, going over, instead of around, the benches and play equipment.

The combination of gymnastic and acrobatic moves, creative yet intentional, had intrigued me. Soon I was trying to copy them, laying claim to that same playground. Stairs with a center railing lead up to the school, high on a hill above the playground. I jog up those stairs, staying to the right of the railing. At the top, I turn and peer into the darkness below.

A lone streetlight casts a glow on the playground. The other lights were broken long ago and never replaced. The play area is a large asphalt square, surrounded by fields on two sides. The hill where I'm standing makes up the third side. A road runs beside the playground and dead ends into a rusty chain-link fence behind a convenience store on the fourth side. The store owners put up the fence to keep kids from going onto their property, but it's in bad shape and does little to keep anyone away.

How long before Thorn gets here? I need to talk to him, to tell him the news I received earlier that made my world tilt. I gaze around, but there's only the four netless basketball hoops perched on posts, like sentinels guarding the old-fashioned play equipment. No Thorn yet.

The images start to come, the same ones that have haunted me for years. A young girl celebrating her sixth birthday. Twirling round and round in a new pink party dress and white sandals with straps that wrap around her ankles. Feeling like a princess.

I know what's coming next, so I jump to my feet and race down the stairs, vaulting back and forth across the center railing until I reach the playground. Trying to escape the pictures playing in my mind, I cross the asphalt and run toward a bench, planting my hand on the back and bringing both legs over for a speed vault.

The swings, bars, slides, and merry-go-round in front of me are well-worn and a bit rusty, but they hold the memories of thousands of children over the years. This equipment is clustered around a newer wooden playset made up of ladders, bridges, slides, and climbing bars that work well for the jumps, flips, and vaults that make up freerunning.

The dim glow of the streetlight illuminates Thorn as he approaches the playground. He's wearing long cotton pajama bottoms, a black tank top, and high-top basketball shoes, same as me, but my shoes are black and white and held together with silver duct tape.

The slight chill of the night air doesn't bother us. We stay warm freerunning. I stride along the border of the playground near Thorn. He falls in beside me and matches his stride to mine. He has his own issues to deal with, so he gets it when I need to run away from the memories that haunt me. Most nights we run in silence in our own version of follow-the-leader.

Passing me, Thorn heads toward a brick wall meant to close off the corner of the playground housing the dumpster and storage shed. It doesn't accomplish that task but gives us a good wall for stunts. Planting his foot hip-high against the wall, Thorn pushes upward off the bricks and performs a perfect back flip. I follow, but back flips are tricky for me. I plant my foot wrong when I push off, sending me downward instead of into the air. I land hard on my bottom.

Thorn drops beside me. "Interesting move."

"Yeah, needs a little work."

"You forgot to drive your knee upward."

I snort. "Obviously."

My mood darkens as I remember why I wanted to talk to him.

Thorn lifts an eyebrow. "What?"

"He called. Mom talked to him."

"Kia ..."

My heart lightens at Thorn's nickname for me. To everyone else, I'm Kiana Scott, but to Thorn, I'm just Kia. Like the car.

"He called," I repeat. "Just like that. Like he has a right." By saying the words aloud, I'm acknowledging it to myself. The *he* isn't my dad, because I don't know who my father is. It's the other he. The one who ruined me—Mom's father.

I jump up and take off, circling the playground with long, strong strides, trying unsuccessfully to slam the door of my mind on the thought of him. Thorn follows me as I weave in and out of the basketball poles, swinging myself in a wide arc on each pole.

I race to the horizontal bars, swing up, and sit. Thorn lands beside me, sweat glistening on his skin. Our arms touch, his white, mine light brown. Thorn calls me dusky.

He tilts his head to the side, studying me. "What does he want?"

I scoot to the edge of the bars and swing my legs back and forth. "Has cancer." I say it fast to cover the tremor in my voice. "Says he wants Mom's support."

"Really?" Thorn tightens his lips, then speaks again. "Her support?"

"So he says." I reach in my pocket and feel the Statue of Liberty souvenir coin my third-grade teacher gave me for getting a 100% on my geography test. I've carried it with me since. Prizes are rare in my world. I rub the coin between my thumb and first finger.

Thorn's eyes narrow. "He expects your mom to do what?"

"Don't know. But now, I'm thinking of what he did all over again." I release the coin and rub the back of my neck.

Thorn gives a quiet laugh. Not the kind that means something's funny ... the other kind. "Like you ever stopped. Like you even could."

I swing my legs harder. "I try."

He turns toward me. "You run."

I shrug one shoulder. "It's what I do best. Run."

Thorn's face is only inches from mine, his warm breath tickling my cheek. "Maybe it's time you face the issue."

If only it were that easy. If only bile didn't rise in my throat thinking about it. "It's too late. It can't be undone. I'll never be a normal teen. Normal was stolen from me."

Thorn looks thoughtful. He runs his hand backward through his closely clipped dark-blonde hair. What can he say? I'm right.

"True ..."

"But?"

"There's always hope."

"Hope for what?"

"A new ending. You can't change the beginning, but you don't have to let him write the ending too."

At Thorn's words, I feel a spark of some emotion I can't name. I don't know what to do or say, so I jump from the bars and cross the playground to the road home. Thorn is behind me as I jog down the street. Two dogs have tipped over a trashcan and are scavenging through the contents. The stench of rotted food invades my senses, making the inside of my nose burn. I speed up, and Thorn keeps pace. We race to my house where I grasp the cool metal porch post and pull myself up, hand over hand, my muscles taut.

I reach the roof. My fingertips grasp the edge. I pull myself up, ignoring the pain as rough shingles bite into my skin. Thorn is right behind me. We sit side by side next to my bedroom window, leaning against the house. My skin prickles from the cool aluminum siding. My tank top isn't warm enough now that we've stopped running, but

I'm not ready to go inside yet.

The clouds part, and points of light blaze above us. Why does the night sky make me long for something I can't even name? I gaze upward and point. "There's Orion. See the three stars in a row? That's his belt."

I glance at Thorn. He's motionless, knees to his chest, arms wrapped loosely around them. His lips are slightly parted, and he gazes upward.

From down the street, a child's cry is followed by yelling and the crash of shattering glass, breaking the spell cast by the expanse of stars. Just another night on Willow Street, a place where people dump their junk curbside until the next pick-up day, so a constant assortment of old tires, appliances, and bathroom fixtures adorn the roadside the way trees and flowers do in other sections of town. A sigh escapes my lips. My surroundings are a reminder that my life has too much debris and not enough flowers.

Thorn turns to me, a question in his eyes.

I take a breath and blow it out slowly. "Why'd he have to call? Isn't it enough that I relive his abuse over and over in my dreams?"

I pull my knees to my chest and clutch them tightly until they start to cramp. I release my grip and stretch my legs. There's another tear in my shoe. I need more duct tape, my solution to most things in my life. But duct tape can't fix everything.

"Maybe he's got regrets," Thorn says.

I don't turn to face him, but I know he's watching me. I can feel it. I huff, air escaping from my nostrils. "Regrets for what he did to me? Not likely. Shouldn't make a difference to me anyway. I'm not six anymore."

"If it didn't make a difference, the memories wouldn't still haunt you."

I pull my legs to my chest and lean forward. "You know what it's like to hide something. To pretend it never happened. My grandfather. Your dad." I turn my head to look at him. "You and me? We both come from a hard place."

Thorn shifts sideways, looking directly at me. "Doesn't change the fact there's a plan for us. Someone bigger than us is orchestrating things."

Thorn's face is illuminated by the stars and a dim streetlight. I look into his shadowed blue eyes, searching my face. I open my mouth, trying to form an answer. This isn't the first time we've had this conversation.

"If there is a God, how could he sit back and watch what my grandfather did to me? What your dad did to you and your mom? What kind of God would let little kids get hurt?"

Thorn looks down and shakes his head. "I don't know the answer to that. But I know I trust him, look to him for courage, for the strength to do what it takes to make things change. Maybe it's time you claim the courage to do what you need to do."

I press my lips together, then exhale. "Like what? Have a chat with my grandfather? Tell him I forgive him for what he did? No thanks."

"No. Not that. But maybe you're meant to finally face it. Start writing your new ending."

I breathe in slowly through my nose and out my mouth. "Why now? I don't even know where to begin."

He turns his head to look at me. "Why not now? Don't let him win."

Heat rushes through me. Thorn doesn't get it. My grandfather has already won. "I can't talk about this more. I need to sleep."

I stand. Thorn looks up at me, but for now the conversation is over. I turn and slip through the open window into my room, then look back and watch as Thorn walks to the edge of the roof. He drops from view, and I hear a soft thud. His shadow disappears into the night.

FREERUNNER

A young adult novel by

Kathy Cassel

Night is Kia's favorite time, when she freeruns to outdistance the memories of abuse she suffered as a young child. But when former reality television star Terrence Jones arrives at their school as the new head track coach, things begin to change in unpredictable ways. Kia tries out for the team to fit in, but just as she's gaining a new sense of normal, her abuser steps back into her life. Not only that, but trouble between team members and coaches cause even more turmoil. Kia soon realizes she has to choose between running from her past or saving a child from the same sort of abuse she suffered. But will she have the courage to do so?

Available Now

at

Amazon.com